THE UNGAINLY WALLFLOWER

WALTZ)ING WITH WALLFLOWERS BOOK 4

ROSE PEARSON

LANDON HILL MEDIA

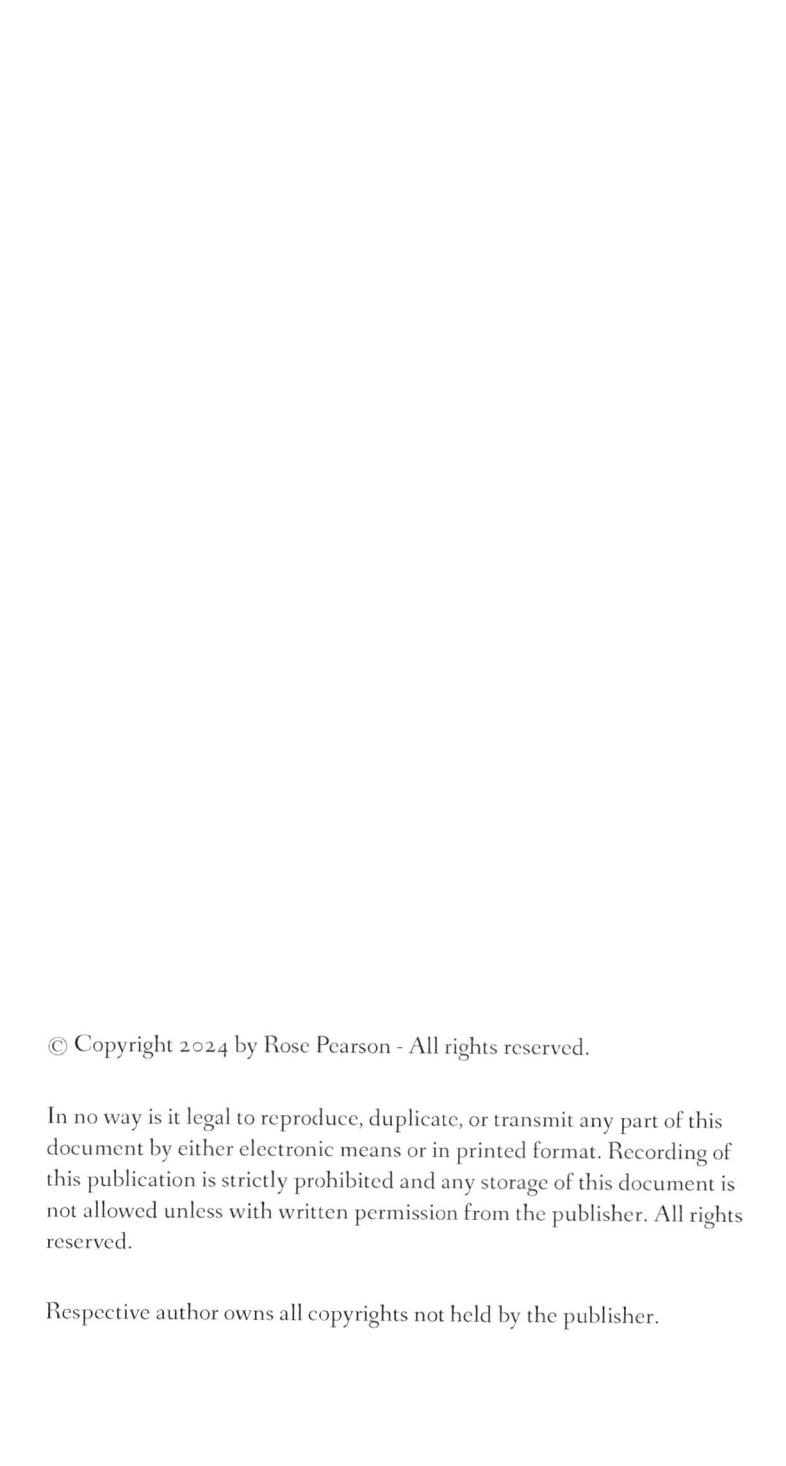

© Copyright 2024 by Rose Pearson - All rights reserved.

In no way is it legal to reproduce, duplicate, or transmit any part of this document by either electronic means or in printed format. Recording of this publication is strictly prohibited and any storage of this document is not allowed unless with written permission from the publisher. All rights reserved.

Respective author owns all copyrights not held by the publisher.

THE UNGAINLY
WALLFLOWER

PROLOGUE

"*E*mma?"

Closing her eyes, Miss Emma Fairley let out a long, slow breath, steadying herself inwardly.

"Yes, Mama?"

"Are you quite ready?"

Recalling what had already happened to her the previous evening, Emma pressed her hands to her cheeks, praying that the embarrassment that had seared through her would not easily return. Given that she had made no answer, Lady Follet practically danced through the door, her eyes glittering with evident delight. She appeared to be more excited than Emma was about the upcoming ball, though that might well be because Emma's older sister appeared to have caught the interest of a high-titled gentleman.

"Whatever is taking you so long?" Lady Follet exclaimed, catching Emma's hand and squeezing it firmly. "You appear to be ready, and the carriage is already here – as is your sister. Martha is desperate for us to make our way to the ball, and I cannot understand why you linger so!"

Emma offered a small smile, though her stomach knotted with tense anxiety which coursed right through her.

"I just want to make certain that everything is quite perfect, Mama."

"So long as you do not stumble over the hem of your gown and fall into Lord Wellbridge's arms again as you did last evening, then all shall be well," her mother said flippantly, waving one hand in Emma's direction before hurrying towards the door. "Now do hurry up. This evening cannot wait!"

Much to her surprise, hot tears formed behind Emma's eyes, and she had to blink furiously to push them away. With only a single sentence, her mother had reminded her of her embarrassment, had thrown it at her, and then reminded her of what was at stake for this evening.

"I do not know what is happening," Emma murmured softly, walking to the door, and trying to steady herself inwardly.

Almost every time she had stepped into society of late, something had occurred that not only embarrassed her but which made her feel so utterly ashamed that she could barely keep her head held high. Thus far, she had stumbled into a group of gentlemen and ladies, had tripped and fallen during one of the dances and into the gentleman's arms, had stepped back and knocked a glass of wine from a lady's hand which had subsequently tumbled over her, had splashed soup onto her gown when someone nudged her elbow and, on one occasion, become too close to a carriage on a rainy day and had become very wet indeed due to the splashing from the wheels.

It seemed that, no matter what she did or where she went, something went wrong. Emma was all too aware that she was garnering a reputation for being clumsy and foolish and, try as she might, she could not seem to escape it. She had told herself that on some occasions, it was not *her* doing, but was due to the failure of others - but the blame for some mishaps certainly sat on her shoulders. However, last evening had not been her foolishness. It had not been any lack of ability to follow the correct steps of the dance, had not been her failure in stepping out when she ought not to have done... but even her mother had not believed her. She had criticized Emma for not practicing enough with the dance master, and had told her how mortified she ought to be... and Emma had felt every single bit of embarrassment seeping down into her bones, just as she felt it now.

I can only hope that nothing untoward will happen, Emma told herself, following her mother down the staircase and towards the door. *Perhaps I shall stay in the shadows and pretend that I am not present, in the hope of causing my family no further hint of shame.*

"*Do* hurry up," Martha exclaimed, pulling up the edge of her gloves as she tapped her foot on the floor in obvious impatience. "You may have no desire to go into society after last evening's fiasco, but I certainly do."

Emma opened her mouth to respond, only to close it again with a snap. Her sister was quite correct, for Emma certainly had no wish to attend another ball. No doubt she would be forced into Lord Wellbridge's company again, due to his interest in her sister, and that would bring further embarrassment with it!

"We are ready now," Lady Follet said with a hurried smile, ushering both girls towards the carriage. "Now do come on. Your father does not like to be kept waiting!"

Emma swallowed, nodded, and then stepped into the carriage, her fears already mounting. What clumsiness would overtake her this evening? How ungainly would she be, and what whispers would the *ton* say of her now?

"Do excuse me."

Emma pressed her lips tight together as she moved forward carefully, making certain not to brush into any ladies or bump the arms of any of the gentlemen. She was nervous about making any sort of mistake, afraid of any sort of mishap that might make the eyes of the *ton* turn their attention towards her again. The ball had gone very well so far, given that she had not caused any accidents or done anything improper so, in that regard, Emma was satisfied. Her sister was busy dancing with various gentlemen and had her waltz already reserved by Lord Wellbridge, the gentleman who seemed eager for her attention. Her mother was busy watching Martha's every step and thus, Emma had though it best to step to the back of the ballroom for a time, so she might hide in the shadows and make certain not to cause any sort of difficulty. The crowd became a little less busy and she was soon able to find her way through until, much to her relief, she found herself at the very back of the room. Turning, she crossed her arms over her chest and let out a slow breath, only for someone to speak to her, causing her to yelp in surprise.

"Good evening. Are you quite all right?"

Emma turned quickly, seeing a young lady smiling back at her.

"I – I am."

"I just wanted to make quite certain that you were not separated from those you care about," the young lady continued, offering her a small smile. "Though perhaps you did not intend to come and stand with the wallflowers?"

Emma blinked in surprise, realizing a little too late that a few young ladies were standing together, though only one or two had their eyes turned in Emma's direction.

"I did not, but that does not trouble me, if that is your concern."

"No?" The young lady's smile grew, her eyes flickering with interest. "I would have thought that most young ladies would do everything they could to step away from wallflowers so that the gentlemen of the *ton* know that they are not one of them!"

"Mayhap I should be one," Emma replied, a little heavily. "I have a deep and heavy struggle and it seems to me at this moment that standing back here, away from my mother, father, and sister, might be the very best thing for me to do. After all, it means that I will not be able to do anything that could cause anyone any embarrassment – including myself!" Seeing the strange look from the young lady, Emma spread out her hands, her cheeks infusing with heat. "I have had difficulty of late in terms of being a little... clumsy, though it has not always been my fault," she said, hastily, wanting to make it clear that she was not entirely to blame for all of the things which had happened. "I do not know what it is that happens, I do not understand what always takes place but, yet, I am now becoming reputed, amongst the *ton,* to be rather ungainly." She closed her eyes. "After what happened last evening, I am quite sure that there will be many a gentleman relieved that I will not dance this evening."

"What do you mean?" the young lady asked, coming a little closer to Emma. "Why would they be relieved?"

Her face still hot, Emma shrugged lightly, seeing that she had no choice but to explain.

"I have trodden on someone's foot and stumbled into the arms of a gentleman during the dance," she explained, all the more embarrassed when the young lady's eyes flared. "Though I will say that someone stood on my heel and tugged my slipper which was why I then lost my footing."

"How dreadful!" the young lady exclaimed, making Emma smile at her fervor. "That is utterly disgraceful. I do hope that you were able to explain that to the gentleman. It is not fair if *you* should take the blame for that."

Emma gave a quiet, tight laugh.

"I am afraid that there was no opportunity for explanation. I found myself embarrassed and too ashamed to speak. Besides which, everyone dancing – and everyone watching – saw it and I could not explain to each of them that what I had done was not my fault!"

The young lady smiled in sympathy.

"I suppose so. All the same, you must know that it is not your doing, and you cannot feel guilty for such things. I would not have you hide away with the wallflowers when there is no need." Her smile grew a little sorrowful. "It is not as though it is a particularly happy situation."

That gave Emma pause. She had always noticed the wallflowers but had never once considered their feelings about being treated in such a way. That was sorrowful indeed, and she could well understand the young lady's disappointment. However, was she not also struggling? Was she not also being shunned by society, being pushed away from those who surrounded her? Their whispers and laughter were almost too much to bear, and her fear when she stepped out into society was growing with every opportunity that came to her. There was almost a pull towards the wallflowers, she had to admit. A pull that was growing, despite the sorrow in the lady's voice.

"I am not in a particularly happy situation myself," she murmured, seeing the young lady's eyes flicker. "Though I am sorry that you are in such a position. I am sure it is not as you thought the Season would be."

The young lady sighed and shrugged.

"It is as must be, I suppose," she said, softly. "I cannot help it. My situation is such that such things are simply meant to be."

"Well, if things continue as they are, I may find myself present here next Season," Emma said, quietly, sharing a smile with the young lady. "But for the moment, I shall have to do my very best not to cause myself any more embarrassment... though whether I shall succeed remains to be seen."

The young lady smiled softly.

"I will pray that I will not see you here next Season," she said, making Emma smile back in appreciation at the kindness of her words. "My very best to you. Despite this, may you have the most successful Season."

CHAPTER ONE

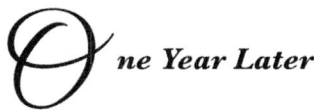ne Year Later

"Your dance card, Miss Fairley?"

Emma watched as her sister handed her dance card to Lord Wellbridge, wondering if this would be the Season when Lord Wellbridge would propose to her sister. Last Season, they had shown a good deal of interest in each other, but Lord Wellbridge had never once suggested courtship or the like though, given that this was now their third ball of the Season and he had danced twice with her at each one, Emma hoped it might soon come about.

She did care for her sister, and did hope that she found happiness. At the same time, there was a faint hope that she might be given a little more attention by their mother, once her sister was betrothed. Thus far, out of the three balls they had attended, Emma had been given very little attention, had barely danced, and had done nothing whatsoever to garner interest from anyone. It was as though her mother had decided that her sister was of greater importance than Emma – though mayhap, she was also still embarrassed by all that had followed Emma last Season.

"And you, Miss Fairley? Should you like to dance?"

Emma smiled in surprise, appreciative of Lord Wellbridge's consideration.

"Yes, that would be wonderful. I thank you."

"You will have to be careful with my sister, however," Martha interjected, as Lord Wellbridge took the dance card from Emma, a laugh in her voice. "She is not inclined to dance with any particular grace!"

Heat rippled up Emma's chest and into her face as she looked directly at her sister, seeing the way that Martha flushed red, catching Emma's eye, and then looked away. Why had she said such a thing as that?

"I am sure it will be a lovely dance," Lord Wellbridge replied, still signing Emma's dance card – much to her relief – and then handing it back to her. "The cotillion, Miss Fairley? I hope that is satisfactory."

"More than satisfactory, I assure you."

Emma managed to smile and then put the dance card back on her wrist, keeping her gaze away from her sister. There was another brief conversation and, shortly thereafter, Lord Wellbridge took his leave.

"Whatever did you say such a thing as that for?" The moment the gentleman stepped away, Emma turned to her sister, the heat in her face turning to tears. "I am aware that I may have been a little clumsy in the previous

Season, but I have danced many dances without any difficulty! Why should you say such a thing as that to Lord Wellbridge? You embarrassed me a great deal."

"Indeed, Martha, that was a little inconsiderate," their mother said, quietly. "I am surprised at you."

As Emma watched, her sister closed her eyes and then dropped her head, though heat still lingered in her cheeks.

"Forgive me," she mumbled, as Emma frowned. "I – I found myself a little jealous. The words slipped from my mouth before I could think of what I was saying."

Instantly, the upset left Emma and she let out a slow breath, shaking her head and turning away from her sister.

"I am not at all interested in pursuing any sort of connection with Lord Wellbridge," she said, softly. "I thought you would have understood that, Martha. I want very much for you to be happy."

Her sister reached out one hand and took Emma's, shaking her head as she did so.

"I am terribly sorry. I did not mean to say such things. My heart is a little pained, given that last Season, we appeared to be so very near to courtship, and yet nothing came of it."

"I am sure something will happen this Season," Emma replied, as their mother nodded fervently. "And if not, then there will be many other gentlemen who want your attention. You will be betrothed by the end of the Season, I am sure of it!"

Her sister gave her a rather watery smile and all of Emma's angst disappeared in an instant, seeing just how upset Martha was. Thus far, Martha had said nothing about Lord Wellbridge to her, and Emma had not had any real understanding of just how sorrowful her sister had been over the gentleman. They were not particularly close as sisters, and Emma found herself regretting that.

"You can be assured of my support," she murmured, as their mother smiled and then beckoned them to walk forward so they might, no doubt, find someone else to talk with and have their dance cards signed. "You can trust me for that, I assure you."

Martha nodded, sniffing lightly, but lifting her chin to keep her expression gentle.

"I thank you, Emma. That does mean a great deal to me."

"But of course."

With a smile, Emma slipped her arm through her sister's and together, they followed their mother.

"Thank you for the dance, Miss Fairley."

Emma managed a smile, her heart slamming hard into her chest repeatedly, given that she had only just finished her dance with Lord Gibson.

"I thank you for it, Lord Gibson. It was most enjoyable."

He offered his arm and Emma took it at once, finding herself flooded with relief that she had been able to dance not only with Lord Gibson but also, prior to that, with Lord Wellbridge, and had done so without falling, slipping, bumping into anyone, or stamping on anyone's toes.

All had gone very well indeed, and she was beginning to believe that this Season might now be a good deal better than the previous one.

"Let me return you to your mother, who I see waiting there."

Lord Gibson gestured to her, and Emma smiled, catching her mother's eye for a moment. Lady Follet looked very pleased indeed which, to Emma's mind, meant that she was delighted with how the evening was going. That gave her more hope, believing that perhaps her mother would be a little more interested in helping her to find a match as well as her sister.

"My Lord, my Lady?"

Emma and Lord Gibson paused as a footman held out a tray for them. Upon it were both glasses of wine and smaller glasses of brandy and Emma, though she would much have preferred to have a glass of water given how hot and thirsty she was after dancing, thought to take a glass of wine. Lord Gibson took a glass of brandy and then released Emma's arm so that she might take a drink also.

"Thank you," she said, reaching for a glass of wine. No sooner had her fingers touched the glass than the footman's arm jerked, as though, somehow, she had startled him. To her horror, she saw the tray tip forward, the glasses beginning to slide and tip towards the edge – and without knowing what she was doing, Emma reached to steady the footman, trying to catch his arm, trying to stop the glasses from falling to the ground.

She did not succeed.

With horror, she saw the glasses fall from the edge of

the tray and then fall directly to the floor. The sound of smashing glass reverberated around the room and though she hurried to step back, liquid from both the wine and the brandy splashed onto her gown and the boots and breeches of Lord Gibson.

The silence that followed made Emma's stomach twist with a sudden fright, dread filling her as she realized that the nightmare which she had dreaded had once more taken hold. She had no idea of how the tray had fallen but yet, every eye was fixed upon her as though she were the one responsible. Her chest grew tight, her breathing quickening as Lord Gibson took a step back from her.

"Whatever happened?" Lady Follet rushed towards her as murmuring began to rush around the room, though everyone still looked at her, with many whispering behind their hands. "What did you do, Emma?"

"I – I did nothing!" Emma protested, aware that her words sounded weak. "It was not my doing. All I did was reach out and take the glass of wine and then the tray fell."

The footman who had dropped the tray was already attempting to pick up some of the glass and was quickly joined by other servants who began to do the same. Heat ran through her as she turned away, stammering an apology to Lord Gibson who, after only a moment, nodded and then turned on his heel, leaving her alone with her mother.

"I did not do this," Emma whispered, though her mother closed her eyes tight, her face rather white. "Mama, I did not! I–"

"I will send for the carriage to take you home," her

mother interrupted, opening her eyes, reaching out, and catching Emma's hand before beginning to pull her away. "There is nothing else for it."

"But what about Martha?" Emma protested, suddenly worried that her sister would suffer for her mistakes. "She ought not to be pulled away."

Lady Follet turned around, coming to a sudden stop.

"You misunderstand me, Emma," she said, firmly. "I am telling you that *you* are returning home. *You* are to prepare for and then retire to bed. I will have the carriage return here to wait for the ball to end. I will certainly *not* punish your sister for your clumsiness."

Emma's heart dropped like a stone.

"I did not do anything, Mama," she said, her voice breaking with emotion, wishing that her mother would believe her. "I do not understand what happened, but I am truly telling you that the only thing I did was take a glass from the tray. I did not fall into him, I did not stumble forward, I did not—"

"I am not interested in any of your excuses!" Lady Follet hissed, grasping Emma's hand again and pulling herself a little closer to Emma. "Do you understand? You have not only embarrassed yourself, but you have also embarrassed me and your father *and* your sister! It is best for us all that you take yourself home and do so at once."

She turned and marched Emma out of the ballroom and into the hall, though Emma's eyes immediately began to fill with tears, her heart aching at the pain her mother's words had caused. Blinking furiously, she found herself outside, seeing her mother speaking to the footman who instantly hurried away.

"I will return to your sister," Lady Follet stated, coming back to Emma as quickly as she could. "There are two footmen here. Stay with them until the carriage arrives and then make your way home."

Emma blinked furiously, her tears returning with a vengeance.

"You are not even going to stand with me?"

"I must be seen with your sister!" Lady Follet exclaimed, throwing up her hands. "I must do what I can to quash the whispers that are surely going to follow you now that this has happened. I will do my utmost to protect Martha from what you have done and, as I have said, it would be best for you to take yourself home and retire to bed." She shook her head, her jaw tight. "Have the maid soak your gown the moment you return home. Let us hope that your father will not have to pay for yet another new gown for you."

With that, she was gone, leaving Emma to stand alone but for those two footmen almost standing guard over her. She watched her mother stalk away from her as though she could not hurry herself away fast enough and, though she tried her utmost to control her tears, she could not prevent them from falling to her cheeks. Dropping her head in the hope of hiding them from the footmen who would, no doubt, whisper about what they had witnessed this evening, Emma felt her heart begin to ache all over again. This Season, which had started off so well, was now falling around her ears in disappointment, disillusion, and confusion, and now, all she could do was return home in disgrace.

CHAPTER TWO

"Good evening, Lord Yeatman."

Frederick smiled and inclined his head.

"We have been friends for many years now, Lord Gibson. I do not think that we need to be so formal!"

Lord Gibson chuckled and stuck out his hand, shaking Frederick's very firmly indeed.

"I suppose that is true. How good to see you again!"

"And in White's," Frederick chuckled, as his friend grinned. "You find me in my favorite place in London, Lord Gibson, and I confess that I have not yet ventured out much into society."

"No?"

Frederick shook his head.

"I much prefer having a few days to myself when I first arrive. It gives me time to consider what it is that I wish to accomplish, and to take note of who else is present!"

"Ah." Lord Gibson tilted his head and looked at him,

a glint in his eye. "Might I ask you if there is anyone in particular that you are attempting to take note of?"

Frederick laughed and shook his head.

"No, you mistake my meaning entirely. I have no particular interest in courting. I am merely interested in who is present, as I can be rather particular with my friendships and the like, as you well know."

Lord Gibson chuckled and then sat down in a chair beside Frederick rather than remaining standing beside him.

"That is something I well remember. I do not think that you considered me a friend until we had been acquainted for at least two years."

"And spent many hours together," Frederick agreed, laughing along with his friend. "Yes, I am afraid I am a little too discerning when it comes to such things. Mayhap I ought to be a little less so, but I find that it is simply a way that I have settled into, and I do not think that I can change any time soon. You know very well how this came about."

Lord Gibson nodded, a solemnity in his expression now.

"Your father."

"Precisely. He was acquainted with Viscount Taylor, thinking him a decent fellow, only of the scandal to not only affect Lord Taylor but also my own father's reputation. Given that my father was inordinately wealthy, the *ton* believed that he funded Lord Taylor's schemes though, of course, he did not."

"Lord Taylor was the guilty one, what with his cheating and brutish behavior," Lord Gibson reminded them both. "He hid it very well, though I was sorry that the scandal affected your own father. That was unfortunate."

"It was."

"But it has led to you being rather discerning, and that is no bad thing, especially since you now carry that burden of wealth," Lord Gibson said quickly. "I think that is probably very wise, given society and those within it. There are many rogues and scoundrels who ought not to be a part of our circles, certainly. And there are mayhap some young ladies who ought to be avoided also!"

Frederick looked back at him in surprise.

"Young ladies? Do you mean those who are widowed and perhaps, a little more free with their attentions?" Catching a footman's attention, he clicked his fingers and ordered a brandy for them both before turning his attention back to his friend. "I am aware that there are more than a few such ladies, though I do not know their names as yet."

Lord Gibson shook his head.

"No, you misunderstand me, though yes, certainly, there *are* some young ladies in the situations you have suggested who ought to be avoided, should one wish to keep a perfectly presentable reputation, which I am aware that you do."

A little puzzled, Frederick frowned.

"Then what do you mean?"

Letting out a long sigh, Lord Gibson winced and then gestured down to his boots.

"My boots are splattered with wine and brandy because of one particular young lady."

"Oh?"

Lord Gibson scowled.

"We were dancing together and, thereafter, I was leading her back to her mother when a footman carrying a tray approached us. For whatever reason, instead of taking one glass, the lady managed to knock the entire tray of drinks onto the floor, and they shattered all over everything."

"And splattered their contents all over you?" Frederick enquired, as Lord Gibson nodded. "Goodness, that was rather unfortunate."

"Yes, it was." Lord Gibson rolled his eyes. "I ought to have been more careful. The young lady in question is known to have something of a clumsy reputation, and I should have been a good deal more cautious in asking her to dance."

Frederick's eyebrows lifted.

"A clumsy reputation?"

Lord Gibson nodded fervently.

"Yes, indeed! She has been tripping over this and knocking over that, injuring this person, and causing various damages - though I do believe that not all of those were her doing." He shrugged. "All the same, there does appear to be an ungainliness about her which seems to have spread from last Season to this."

"Then I shall have to be cautious!" Frederick laughed, taking the brandy from the footman, and handing it to Lord Gibson. "Might I ask the name of this fearsome creature?"

Lord Gibson took a sip of his brandy and then let out a small, contented sigh.

"A Miss Fairley," he said, waggling one finger in Frederick's direction. "Though not the elder one but the younger."

"I see." Frederick took a sip from his glass and then let out a slow breath, smiling contentedly as a feeling of great relief settled over him. "I shall make certain to stay away from the lady, then. I do not want to end up in any sort of difficult situation because of her, though I do pity someone who is so very ungainly. That must be rather trying."

"Trying for those around her, certainly!" Lord Gibson laughed, as Frederick chuckled quietly. "Now, you say that you are not here to consider courtship and such things. Does that mean that you are only here to enjoy yourself?"

Frederick nodded.

"For a short while, yes. The estate is doing well, and the crops are likely to be very successful this year, so my tenants and servants tell me. Therefore, I thought to give myself a little time away from my estate to simply enjoy myself with old friends and new. Though," he continued, with a small shrug, "if a young lady comes to my attention, I will not reject the idea. It is a responsibility of every titled gentleman to marry."

Lord Gibson rolled his eyes.

"My mother continues to plague me with such words," he said, making Frederick laugh. "*She* is why I have come to London. She will not remove to the Dower House until I am wed – such is tradition – and I can barely abide her presence for more than a few minutes for the conversation *always* turns to young ladies and whether I am soon to provide her not only with a daughter-in-law but also a grandchild. She has always been foolish in doting upon children in the way she does. To her, it is less about the heir and more about the sound of children's laughter within the house!"

Frederick smiled quietly.

"I do not think that is such a terrible thing," he said, seeing Lord Gibson's eyebrows lift. "Though I can understand that it must be rather trying to hear it over and over again."

"And how does your own mother fare?"

That sent a small stab of pain into Frederick's heart.

"She has not returned from my sister's house as yet," he said, seeing his friend smile sympathetically. "Ever since my father passed away some three years ago, she has not felt quite at home in the estate. When she received the invitation to visit Charlotte and Lord Hartwood, that was the first time I had seen her smile in many a month. The truth is, I do not think that she will return to live at the estate again. When I marry, she may wish to remove to the Dower House, or she may continue to reside at the Hartwood estate. I think my sister is more than contented to have her present."

"That is a blessing, I suppose, though I am sorry for the pain that such a loss brings," came the reply. "I would much prefer that, I think, than to care very little for the passing of one's spouse." He wrinkled his nose. "I do not think that I have ever seen my mother happier than the day my father was buried. There was no affection between them."

Frederick shifted in his chair, finding himself a little uncomfortable. He had never truly given much thought to his prospects and desires when it came to matrimony, but one thing was for certain; he had no eagerness to be wed to someone who did not care one jot for him!

"I do not think that I would demand love from my betrothed," he said slowly, finding himself being a little more honest with his friend than he had intended, "but I should certainly like an interest to be there." Seeing Lord Gibson frown, Frederick spread out one hand, the other still holding his brandy glass. "What I mean by that is to say that I would not like to have a bride who cared nothing for me in the least, and was only marrying me out of obligation or by arrangement."

Slowly, his friend began to nod, his gaze becoming thoughtful.

"I believe that I understand and yes, I think that I should agree with you there. After all, when one marries, it is meant to be for a good many years, should God's blessing be on you, and I should think it would be more of a dire struggle to have a bride who has no interest in spending even the smallest amount of time in your company!" That thoughtful look was soon chased away by a broad, bright smile as a twinkle came into Lord Gibson's eye. "Though why we are even talking of or considering such things, I do not know, given that you have no real intention of pursuing it and neither do I!"

Frederick chuckled, the somber moment gone from them.

"Indeed, you are quite right. Goodness, here I am sitting in White's, a brandy in my hand, and in fine company, permitting myself to think the most foolish things and bringing my spirits down low. How ridiculous that is!"

"Indeed," his friend said, firmly. "We must give ourselves happier things to talk about. Tell me, are you going to be throwing any balls, soirees, or dinners while you are in London?"

Frederick blinked.

"I have not thought about doing so, but I suppose I could consider it."

"Though you would, no doubt, have to be very cautious and careful as to whom you would invite," Lord Gibson chuckled, making Frederick laugh again. "That may prove a little difficult for you, I think."

"So long as I do not invite that very clumsy young lady... what was her name again?"

Lord Gibson laughed aloud, his eyes twinkling.

"Miss Fairley?"

"Yes, that is right," Frederick grinned. "So long as I do not invite Miss Fairley, then I think any dinner party would go very well indeed, would it not?"

This had his friend dissolving into laughter and, though Frederick joined in, he found himself still a little intrigued by the idea of meeting Miss Fairley. She certainly had made an impression upon Lord Gibson, and though it might very well not be the right impression, Frederick was still a little curious as to who this young lady might be.

CHAPTER THREE

"It was *most* embarrassing. I do not know what we are to do!" Emma closed her eyes, her whole body trembling just a little as she listened to her mother and father discussing her as though she was not present. "The whole tray of drinks, Follet!" her mother exclaimed, as though he – and Emma, for that matter – did not already know what had taken place. "They all came crashing down and Lord Gibson's breeches and boots were soaked with both wine and brandy!"

"It was not as bad as all that, Mama," Emma protested, seeing both of her parents turn their attention to her at once, though Lady Follet's expression was rather dark. "And as I have said to you before, it was not my doing! The footman jerked forward, though I do not know why, and the tray fell just as I had picked up my glass."

Her father sighed and rubbed one hand over his eyes.

"I would believe you, my dear," he said, softly, "if it was not for the fact that such things have happened before. Last Season was something of a disaster when it came to your... ungainliness and I am sorry to say that it appears to be the very same issue arising again."

Emma wanted to weep, such was her frustration and her upset, though she managed to steady herself enough to keep her tears from falling.

"I swear to you, Father, it was not my doing. I understand why you might believe that I did something to cause it, but I promise you, it was not so."

Lord Follet sighed again and looked back to his wife, leaving Emma to search their faces, but both of their expressions were inscrutable.

"I think that it would be best if you stayed back from society a little," her father said eventually, looking back at Emma with something of a resigned expression. "It is for the best."

"Best for whom?" she asked quickly, her throat beginning to ache. "Best for you, so that I would not have the chance to embarrass you both any further?" When her father did not respond, but rather simply looked back at Lady Follet, Emma's heart tore apart. It was not for her benefit, then, but rather so that her mother, father, and sister might be free of her. Closing her eyes, Emma let her tears fall, though neither her mother nor father came to comfort her. Rather, they simply looked at her with a steadiness that spoke of a firmness in their decision. She was to be shunned, then, even by her own family. "You want me to stand with the wallflowers," Emma continued when neither of them said a word. "Is that your desire? That I will hide away with them?"

Lady Follet's eyes lifted in evident consideration of such an idea.

"I confess, I had not thought of that. I actually was considering whether or not it would be best for you to remain at home, but I think that standing with the wallflowers would be a good idea. It would mean that you could still be present, but a little less... obtrusive."

The tears continued to fall but Emma wiped them away, trying to steady herself. "You would both be contented with that, then? You would be glad to see me standing alone?"

"You would not be alone!" Lady Follet exclaimed delightedly, as though *she* was the one who had come up with such an idea. "You would be standing with other young ladies who could keep you company and you would still have the opportunity to stand up with various gentlemen should they be interested in dancing with you. You would not lack conversation and–"

"Gentlemen do not dance with wallflowers, Mama!" Emma cried, her tears returning with a vengeance. "That is why they are called wallflowers! They adorn the sides of the ballroom, but never stand up in the middle of the room! They are largely ignored and forgotten and that is the fate that you would be resigning me to!"

"I think that you are being a little dramatic, Emma." Lord Follet cleared his throat and then folded his arms across his chest. "It is a wise suggestion to stand with the wallflowers. Would you prefer to be left at home?"

"I would prefer to be given as much consideration as Martha!" Emma exclaimed, getting to her feet. "I have told you repeatedly that none of this was my doing, but you do not believe me! You turn your face from me and decide that I have to stand aside so that you can focus your attention on Martha. Am I not your daughter also?"

Lady Follet put out her hands on either side and then let them drop, lifting her shoulders as she did so.

"I understand that you might find this difficult, Emma, but it is for the best, as we have said. Yes, you are our daughter, but it would be good for society to forget about you for a short while. It would improve your standing and when you return to London next Season, you will find yourself in a better situation."

"If we return," Lord Follet said, his tone dark. "Listen to me, Emma. Either you do as you are told, or you will *not* return to London next Season."

Lady Follet turned to her husband with a wide-eyed look.

"You mean to say that she would be a spinster?"

"I would be willing to find her a suitable match," Lord Follet said quietly, turning to look at his wife. "I have a cousin, as you recall, who is in need of a bride. He is a good deal older than Emma, which is why as yet, I have not considered him but–"

"Please, do not put me to that fate!" Emma protested, tears beginning to burn in her eyes again. "I will do as you ask."

Her father gave her a curt nod, a small, satisfied smile on his face which Emma felt cut right through her. She sat back down, her hands in her lap, and her head lowering as she closed her eyes tightly against the flood of tears behind them. Her parents continued to talk with one another as though she were absent and Emma's heart sank low, her spirits diminishing until she felt herself weak and tired. There was nothing else for her to do but to agree with her father and mother that she would stand with the wallflowers, that she would *become* a wallflower and refrain from stepping out into society again.

There was nothing else for her this Season – and perhaps not even next Season, should her father decide that it was pointless to put her back in amongst society to find a match there. Her future was bleak, her heart broken and nothing but sorrow awaiting her.

"Good evening." Emma clasped her hands in front of her, looking at the young ladies standing together. "Might I ask if I would be permitted to stand with you?"

The young lady looked back at her, a smile of recognition on her face.

"But of course!" The smile quickly faded as she took in Emma's expression. "You are troubled. I am sorry for that." She bobbed a quick curtsey. "Miss Simmons, if you please."

"Miss Emma Fairley," Emma replied, as the young lady turned and beckoned to another to come closer.

"And this is Lady Frederica."

"It is my pleasure to meet you both." Emma tried to smile though her eyes were still sore from the tears she had cried the previous day. "It seems that I am to stand here with you both, if that would be all right? I do not have anywhere else to go."

"But of course." Miss Simmons smiled gently and

then stepped back so that Emma might come a little closer. "I am sorry for whatever has happened to place you here."

Emma closed her eyes and shook her head.

"My father and mother believe that I am the clumsiest, most ungainly person in all of London, even though I have done my utmost to convince them that it is not always my doing. After what happened recently, it seems as though my parents have decided that I must stay away from both them and my sister so that she might have a Season without interruption."

Lady Frederica and Miss Simmons looked at one another.

"Might I ask what happened?" Lady Frederica asked. "You see, as wallflowers, we are not always privy to the goings-on in society."

Wincing, Emma told them the truth and found herself growing hot with embarrassment all over again. Her two new friends looked at each other and then smiled sympathetically.

"We believe you," Miss Simmons said, gently. "I am sorry that you have been treated in such a way, however. That must be very painful."

Emma looked away, her throat tightening again.

"It is the lesser of two evils, I suppose. My father has suggested a potential match with a cousin of his who is almost of an age with my father himself! If I do not do as he has asked this Season, then that is what will be waiting for me… either that or spinsterhood, forced upon me by my parents." Tears burned behind her eyes, and she dropped her shoulders heavily. "So, it seems as though I shall be a wallflower for this Season at least. Though I am most grateful for your welcome," she finished, managing to look at them both again. "Thank you, Miss Simmons, Lady Frederica."

"But of course." Lady Frederica smiled and lifted her shoulders in a half shrug. "You are not alone here, at least. That is something which is a little encouragement, I hope."

"It is." Emma forced a smile and tried to push aside the heavy sadness which clung to her soul. "With you both, I am sure that I will not find the Season lonely, at least, and that is a good thing indeed."

CHAPTER FOUR

Frederick Marsham, Viscount Yeatman, cleared his throat, lifted his chin, and walked into the ballroom. He did not like the fact that there was a tight tension within his stomach, but it was the first time he had set foot into any sort of social occasion since his arrival in London. It was not that he feared not knowing anyone present, but more that he did not want to be swamped by acquaintances all wishing to speak with him. He preferred to look around the room, amble around it slowly, and thereafter, begin conversations with friends or acquaintances. Having too many people to deal with at once only brought on a headache.

Clasping his hands behind his back, he nodded to one or two people and then turned sharply, making his way to the edge of the room rather than making for the center, where so many others would be. Those within the *ton*, on the whole, sought to keep company with as many others as possible, and would seek to be seen and to be noticed by others, whereas Frederick was quite the opposite. Large crowds did not interest him.

"You are not going to hide away already, are you?" Frederick turned sharply, wondering at the interruption, only to see Lord Pleasance grinning at him. "Lord Gibson pointed you out the moment you stepped into the room," his old friend said, reaching out to shake Frederick's hand as Frederick beamed in delight at seeing him. "We are both very well aware of your dislike of large crowds, however, so when he stated that you would be hiding, you cannot imagine our mirth when we saw you attempt to do precisely that!"

"I am not hiding," Frederick laughed, rolling his eyes. "But I am not seeking out company yet, that is all."

Lord Pleasance chuckled.

"Still a little cautious, are we?"

"Not cautious but careful, yes," Frederick agreed, quietly, shrugging lightly. "There are too many rogues and charlatans and I only have one reputation."

"Very true." Tilting his head, Lord Pleasance studied Frederick for a moment. "What if we were to invite you to dinner? My wife hopes to throw a society dinner very soon, and I can assure you that it will be only the very best of people invited."

"I should be honored!" Frederick exclaimed, having no desire for his friend to think that *he* would be shunned just because of Frederick's cautiousness. "There is nothing that would prevent me from attending, I assure you."

"Wonderful." Lord Pleasance gestured back to where Lord Gibson was standing. "Now, do you wish to come and talk with us? Or are you to walk around the room a little more first?"

"I should like to walk, I think, but I will come back to you." Frederick smiled, his friend nodding in clear understanding of what it was that Frederick desired to do. "Thank you, Lord Pleasance."

"But of course."

Frederick turned and continued to walk at the edge of the room, taking slow steps and taking everything in. There were young ladies gathered together, with mothers and chaperones standing nearby. He saw gentlemen glancing towards certain groups of ladies, then talking together and laughing – though some of the looks on their faces were not at all pleasant, which made Frederick frown. Thereafter, there were other gentlemen and ladies talking together, walking towards the center of the ballroom where they were about to dance.

Dance? Frederick considered for a moment, his steps so slow that he was barely ambling along. *Should I like to dance this Season? It has been some time since I have done that, and I must wonder if I remember how to do it!*

"Excuse me, sir!"

Frederick blinked rapidly, turning his head from where he had looked back at the dance floor and finding himself looking into the face of a young lady who was now a few steps back from him.

"I beg your pardon?"

"You almost walked into us," said a second lady, her face set into a disgruntled expression.

Frederick frowned and then stepped back, lifting his hands in defense.

"I am so sorry. I did not realize."

The two ladies stood together, and Frederick took them in, seeing how they glanced at each other and then frowned. Evidently, he had done them some great wrong, though he did not fully understand how. He had simply been distracted for a few moments.

"We are aware that we are hidden in the shadows, but we are still able to be seen, are we not?" The first lady spoke, looking at him with a slight tilt to her chin, her hazel eyes searching his face. "Wallflowers are still worthy of respect, sir."

In that one moment, Frederick realized exactly what the problem was. He had walked into two young ladies, both of whom were wallflowers and, therefore, generally ignored by society. In doing as he had done, he had added pain to their already difficult situation.

"I am truly sorry," he said, putting one hand to his heart. "I was distracted by watching the dancing."

Again, the two ladies glanced at each other, though one of them shrugged lightly as though to say she did not think that there was anything more that they needed to say. The other, the second, gave a slight sniff.

"Very well," she said, gesturing back to the dance floor. "Let us not keep you, sir."

"Viscount Yeatman." Frederick did not know what it was about these two young ladies, or why he felt himself desirous of giving them his name and title, but there was something about the two of them and the situation they were presently in that caught his attention. "Might I ask for your names also?"

"Our names?" The first young lady, the one whose

hair shone like copper, Frederick noticed, sounded rather surprised. "Why should you want to do that?"

"It is not the correct way of being introduced, I know, but all the same, I should like it," Frederick said, quietly. "After my rude manner, I should like it to be introduced so that I might apologize properly."

He smiled gently, but the two young ladies did not smile with him. The first one was still frowning and the second was studying him as if she were not entirely sure what it was that he genuinely wanted.

"Very well," the first said slowly, her eyes a little narrowed. "What say you?"

She turned to her friend who, after a moment, nodded.

"I am Lady Frederica," the first said, steadily.

"And I Miss Fairley," came the reply from the second, who folded her arms across her chest when Frederick's eyebrows lifted in recognition of her name. "Does that satisfy you, Lord Yeatman?"

Frederick nodded but said nothing, searching his mind for why that name rang around his mind and told him that he already knew of this lady. They had never met, he was sure, for he would have recognized her face, and then surely would have known her title, so why was it that he knew of her?

It came back to him in a flurry, his eyes flaring as he remembered Lord Gibson and his story about a very clumsy young lady who had knocked a tray of drinks down upon him and upon herself also. *That* was how he knew her name.

"Lord Yeatman?" Lady Frederica's eyebrow arched.

"Are you quite all right? Has something surprised you? Or are you wondering what it is that has made us two young ladies become wallflowers?"

Frederick shook his head, trying to find a way to explain what he had realized without doing anything or saying anything to insult the lady.

"It is only that I have just now remembered that one of my friends had mentioned you before, Miss Fairley," he said, gesturing to her and trying to smile in the hope that she would not ask him anything more. "That is all."

Miss Fairley's expression immediately darkened.

"Your friend?" she asked, her tone rather crisp now. "Might I ask his name?"

"It is of no consequence," Frederick replied, shrugging. "Now, might I ask–"

"I have no doubt that whoever this friend is, he did not speak favorably of me," Miss Fairley interrupted, taking a small step closer to him. "Might you tell me the name of your friend, Lord Yeatman?"

Seeing that there was nothing else to be said or done, other than to give her the name, Frederick cleared his throat and kept his smile fixed in place.

"My friend is Lord Gibson, Miss Fairley," he said, seeing how she closed her eyes briefly and then pressed her lips tight together. "Forgive me for my surprise and confusion upon hearing your name and realizing thereafter how I knew of you. I do hope that–"

"And, no doubt, Lord Gibson has told you everything about me and told you about what took place." Again, Miss Fairley interrupted, but her face was slowly beginning to turn scarlet, her hazel eyes sparking bright.

"And now you know of my supposed reputation, I presume?"

Frederick did not know what to say. The truth was that yes, he recalled everything that Lord Gibson had told him about the lady, right down to the very detail of how much brandy and wine had gone onto Lord Gibson's boots.

"I – I do not think that the *ton* is particularly kind in what they say about those within it, Miss Fairley." She looked at him and then shook her head, keeping silent, but clearly communicating with him that what he had said had not answered her question. Somehow, it was clear that she knew he was not telling her everything. She already knew the truth without him having to express it. "I – I shall take my leave of you now," he continued, finding himself more than a little embarrassed as he turned away. "It was my pleasure to be introduced to you both and again, my apologies for my lack of consideration and attention."

Not a word came from either lady and, though Frederick turned and began to walk away, he could feel their sharp gazes boring into him. He made his way quickly back the way he had come, suddenly eager to find his friends simply so that he might rid himself of his embarrassment through general conversation.

So that is Miss Fairley, he mused, spying Lord Gibson and Lord Pleasance talking together. *I did not expect her to be so beautiful.*

That thought stopped him short, and he came to a complete stop, his eyes flaring wide. Yes, he had taken note of both of the young ladies, but Miss Fairley, with her copper hair and hazel eyes, had obviously caught his attention.

Shaking his head, Frederick threw his thoughts aside and continued towards his friends. It was not as though Miss Fairley was the only beautiful young lady in the room and, besides that, he was not considering any young lady at present, was he? With a nod to himself, Frederick made his way to his friends and within the next few minutes, threw all consideration of Miss Fairley away completely.

CHAPTER FIVE

*E*mma sighed and leaned back against the wall, aware that she was of no more significance to those present than the paintings on the wall above her. These last two weeks had been a heavy weight upon her heart, and she had found herself growing more and more despondent with every day that passed. The wallflowers had added to their number and, though she was glad of company, she was sorrowful over her lack of presence in amongst society.

"You look a little sorrowful this evening." Miss Simmons smiled as she came to stand beside Emma. "What troubles you?"

"Aside from being a wallflower?" Emma asked, a little wryly. "I knew that it would be difficult, but I find it more than a little sorrowful to see my sister being guided away by my mother while I am directed to the edge of the room." She sighed heavily, aware that her friend would understand exactly what she was talking about. "This is now the sixth ball I have attended in the last two weeks and the sixth ball where I shall spend many hours watching everyone dancing rather than dancing myself." Her lips pursed for a moment. "Not that I did that very well."

"Though as you have told me, it was not always your doing."

"No, it was not," Emma agreed, her smile a little sad. "Not that it makes any particular difference now."

"I too wish it were different," Miss Simmons agreed, quietly, her eyes and her voice holding the same longing as was in Emma's heart. "But what can be done? At least, for the moment, we have each other."

"Though Miss Bosworth does not seem to be the least bit pleased at having to join us," Emma replied, her gaze snagging on the newest wallflower who had her arms folded and her brows furrowed, standing only a short distance away from both herself and Miss Simmons. "It will take time, I suppose, but she will settle into the way of things soon."

"Mayhap." Miss Simmons tilted her head. "I find Miss Bosworth to have a very strong resolve. I do not know what it is that she intends, but she certainly has no thought of remaining a wallflower!"

Emma's lips curved.

"I do not know what she thinks can be done about it," she replied, softly. "Once you are a wallflower, the *ton* sees you as nothing other than that, regardless of what you might hope."

"That is very true, sadly," Miss Simmons sighed, leaning back against the wall beside Emma and looking out at the crowd who, Emma presumed, were all enjoying the ball while they were not. "It also pains me that my family are so willing to push me back. That is one of my greatest sufferings."

"As it is mine." Emma glanced at her friend, aware of the ache in her heart, and understanding that Miss Simmons shared it. "Though there is one positive outcome from all of this, I must confess."

"Oh?" Miss Simmons' eyebrows lifted. "Might you tell me?"

Emma found herself laughing, making Miss Simmons' confusion grow.

"The only good thing I can see from all of this is that I have not managed to stumble into anyone, I have not knocked a glass of wine across anyone, I have not bumped into someone, I have not embarrassed myself by my ineptness and I have not brought any sort of shame to my family. *That* must be a good thing."

Miss Simmons did not laugh. She did not even smile. Instead, she turned to face Emma a little more and tilted her head just a little.

"Though that is interesting, is it not?" she said slowly, as Emma frowned, not understanding what it was that her friend meant. "It is interesting that you have not had any difficulties in that regard since you have become a wallflower."

Emma wrinkled her nose.

"There is no real surprise there," she stated. "I have not had the opportunity to do any such thing, have I? I am not dancing, I am not conversing with people, I am not–"

"All the same, would you not expect that ineptness,

as you call it, to have followed you even into this situation?" Miss Simmons pulled her lips to one side for a few moments, her eyes still fixed on Emma's. "I would have thought that, given what you have described, I would have *seen* you stumble or trip or do something that would be in line with what you have told me."

Considering this, Emma let herself frown, finally understanding what Miss Simmons meant.

"I have always said that not all that happened was my doing."

"What if none of it was your doing?"

Emma opened her mouth to respond, only for a sudden exclamation to catch her attention. She and Miss Simmons turned to see none other than Miss Bosworth coming towards them, a determined glint in her eyes.

"Miss Bosworth" she asked, as Lady Alice and Lady Frederica came to join them, gathering the full group together. "Is there something the matter?"

Miss Bosworth nodded.

"Yes. Something is wrong."

Emma blinked, glancing at Miss Simmons, but her friend was looking at Miss Bosworth.

"Might I ask what it is?"

Miss Bosworth lifted her chin.

"I am tired of being a wallflower."

Giving a small smile to Lady Alice, Emma put out her hands.

"I believe that we all are."

"I would agree," Miss Simmons added, quietly. "But what can be done?"

Emma watched the smile that crossed Miss

Bosworth's face. It was not one which brought light to her eyes but rather a firmness to her expression. Her stomach dipped. What was it that Miss Bosworth wanted to say?

"Listen to me, all of you," Miss Bosworth began, her voice low but commanding. "Here we are, all standing here at the back of the ballroom without hope of stepping out to dance, without the expectation of good company or the like – and for what reason? None of us have done anything worthy of condemnation. We have been pushed aside by society but that does not mean that we have to remain as we are."

"I do not understand what you mean. We are wallflowers. What more can we expect?" Lady Alice asked as Emma watched, listening rather than interjecting. Her heart told her that there was something significant here, but she did not want to ask questions – not as yet.

Miss Bosworth smiled, but her eyes flicked from one of them to the other, a steely look within them.

"We do not have to do as society expects of us, as I have only just said to you. The *ton* states that wallflowers must stand at the back of the room, silent and unimposing. I say that we do not have to do as they demand. Instead, we might walk, two or three together, about the ballroom, in amongst the guests, and seek to be seen and to be noticed. It might not change a great deal about our situation, but it will make us feel more significant, will it not? It will make certain that we are not forgotten! Even if society thinks we ought not to do anything akin to such a thing, why should it matter? We are already wallflowers. Do we truly wish to act as they demand? Do we wish to shrink back, to hide ourselves away and sink back into the darkness?"

Emma frowned.

"My parents expect me to be forgotten. They do not *want* to see me walking through the ballroom or catching the attention of others."

"But how do *you* feel, Miss Fairley?" Miss Simmons asked, softly. "The *ton* – and your parents – cannot censure us more than it has already done, surely?"

A sudden flare of hope rushed up through Emma's frame.

"I have found myself more than a little despondent of late, I confess. I know that my parents and my sister are very happy indeed, but I have felt myself... lost."

"Of course you have." Miss Bosworth spread out her hands. "Do you not wish for that to change?"

Emma nodded slowly, beginning to understand what it was that Miss Bosworth meant.

"Yes, I do."

"We could stand together in the *center* of the ballroom and converse as so many others do." Turning to Emma, Miss Simmons reached out and gripped her hand. "We do not have to hide here, do we? We could stand in amongst the other guests and talk together, even if no one else wishes to talk to us. What could be wrong with that?"

"There is nothing wrong with that," Miss Bosworth stated firmly, that determination in her voice which only added to the hope that Emma felt within herself. "It will take gumption, certainly, but I, for one, am quite determined to step out and behave just as I please. Society might continue to call me a wallflower, but I will not behave as one."

"And if she will not, then mayhap I ought not to either," Miss Simmons murmured, catching Emma's attention. "What do you think?"

Aware that her heart had quickened, Emma considered for a few moments, sensing a sudden uncertainty rising within her.

"My mother and father would have something to say. I fear that they would be very displeased and, given all that has happened, I am concerned that the clumsiness and ungainliness would continue to chase me once I stepped back into society."

"I do not think that it shall," Lady Frederica said, confidently. "You have friends with you now, do you not?"

Emma nodded slowly, biting her lip, aware that her worries were still very much present. She was being torn in two directions, eager to step back into society and yet afraid of what would happen – and what would be said – if she did.

"I do not know what my mother would think." Miss Simmons turned to Lady Alice before glancing at Emma. "I fear what she would think."

"I can understand that," came the reply, "but I think that we must consider what it would be like if we remained here rather than risking our parents' upset."

Emma frowned at that thought. She certainly did not want to continue as a wallflower, hiding back in the shadows, ignored, and forgotten. Was that enough for her to force herself to do something different from what society – and her own parents – expected?

Miss Bosworth nodded.

"My own mother might also have something to say on the matter. But if I walk with my friends through the ballroom, then I am not alone, I am not without company. There can be nothing said against that in terms of propriety."

"Especially since they have been quite contented for us to stand together alone," Emma added. "They have never been concerned about propriety in that regard."

Miss Simmons glanced at her.

"That is true."

"It is very true," Lady Alice agreed, looking around at them all. "Come, my dear friends, let us be brave. What is better? To stay here, hiding away, pushed aside and ignored? Or to be bold and to step out into the center of the room with the other guests, forcing them to take note of us?"

Courage began to overtake Emma's fear as she caught the determination in Lady Frederica's eyes, and then watched Miss Simmons let out a slow breath as she closed her eyes. "We will be together. We will always have someone with us."

"Precisely," Miss Bosworth stated, smiling.

"And who knows?" Lady Alice shrugged and smiled, though it was a little lackluster. "Mayhap a gentleman will take notice of us!"

Miss Simmons' eyes widened as Emma's doubts immediately began to grow.

"But we are wallflowers?" What will they care for that?"

"It is impossible to tell what might happen, is it not?" Lady Alice smiled again and, this time, it held no fear, no hint of doubts. "Not every gentleman will ignore us, I am sure of it. We may even get to dance! But if we stay here, as we are expected to do, we have no hope at all."

"I – I think I can do it." Miss Simmons looked at Emma, a smile beginning to catch the edge of her mouth. "I know you have the same fears as me, Miss Fairley, as regards our parents. What do you think?"

Emma tried to steady herself, feeling her whole body tingling with a sudden awareness of what they were about to do – and what no wallflower had ever thought to do before. Her eyes strayed to Miss Bosworth as Lady Frederica had taken her arm, clearly already determined that they were going to step out regardless of what the others decided. She was afraid, she realized. Afraid that this would do a great deal more damage to her reputation – and that the clumsiness which had pursued her before would do so again.

"I will." Lady Alice moved forward and took Miss Bosworth's other arm, then looked at Emma and Miss Simmons. "Come, my friends, let us go out together!"

Turning her attention to Miss Simmons, Emma swallowed hard and then nodded, seeing the way her friend's eyes flared in hope.

"Miss Simmons, I think that I can set aside my concerns and walk with the other wallflowers out to the center of the room, to talk to each other and smile and make our presence known. Will you walk with me?"

Miss Simmons hesitated and then, with a nod, stepped forward and took her arm.

"Yes, I shall."

Emma's heart leaped and she turned, watching as Miss Bosworth, Lady Alice and Lady Frederica began to step away from the wall of the ballroom, stepping out into the light and away from the darkness. Despite her worry, despite her fears, Emma followed them, feeling Miss Simmons' arm tighten on hers just a little, clear evidence that she too was feeling a little uncertain.

"It will be difficult, but we can do it," she whispered, as Miss Simmons offered a slightly frightened smile. "All we need to do is walk together, stop in the middle of the crowd, and begin to talk, just as anyone else might do." She looked at Miss Simmons again, taking a deep breath, and as she let it out again, smiled. "What could be easier?"

CHAPTER SIX

Frederick sighed to himself as he looked out of the window to the London street. It was full of carriages and progress was rather slow indeed. Frederick rolled his eyes to himself and then let out another sigh, suddenly aware of how filled with ennui he was.

That was an unusual feeling, for him.

He had been in London now for nearly a month and had, of course, continued with his determination to be cautious and careful as regards his friends and acquaintances. He had stayed at the back of the ballroom for the most part, and been slow to join in with conversation. He had enjoyed his evenings at White's, once whatever social occasion he had joined came to an end, for in that particular establishment, he did not have to worry about a large crush of people or being overwhelmed by those wishing to speak with him. There had been invitations to one or two dinner parties, but the only one he had accepted was Lord Pleasance's invitation - which dinner was due to occur this evening.

What was he to do until then?

Frederick frowned and ran one hand over his chin. He was, in fact, a little lost for ideas as to how he might fill his time. He normally gave so much of his time and energy to making sure that he was surrounded by only the best company, it did not give him a great deal of time to enjoy society's offerings.

Am I being too cautious?

Frederick bit the edge of his lip and then turned away from the window. He knew exactly where all those carriages were going – they were on their way to the fashionable hour, and that meant Hyde Park. The Park itself would soon be crawling with gentlemen and ladies, all making their way there so that society might see them present. Frederick desired to stay away from all of that, to hide from it all but, at the same time, he had to consider the fact that he was lacking in anything to do.

"Should I go?"

Murmuring aloud, Frederick tilted his head and wandered back across the room, considering. What else was there for him to do here? He could sit and write a few letters, deal with some business matters and the like, but that did not offer him any real enjoyment, and nothing was particularly pressing. There was the dinner this evening, which he was looking forward to, but that was still many hours away. What else was there for him to do?

Letting out a slow breath, Frederick pushed one hand through his hair, then turned and walked back to the window to look out at the carriages again. The reasons for his caution were well founded, for there were so many gentlemen and ladies not known to him that he feared that his reputation might be affected if he were to become closely acquainted with someone who was of an unsavory disposition. These characters were not always revealed until much later, Frederick understood, having witnessed what had happened to his father. All the same, he considered, the thought of sitting at his desk and choosing – yet again – not to be in company, was beginning to grow a little wearisome upon his soul.

"Mayhap I should go, even if only for a short while," he considered aloud, nodding half to himself as though to determine that yes, this was what he would do, despite his uncertainties. "It cannot be as bad as sitting here alone!"

With another nod, Frederick turned on his heel and hurried to the door, wondering if he was presentable enough already or if he needed to change. Calling for his valet *and* for the carriage to be brought around, Frederick went to his bedchamber, preparing to make his way to the fashionable hour for the very first time this Season.

∽

"Good afternoon, Lord Yeatman. I did not think that I would find you here!"

Frederick smiled and inclined his head.

"Good afternoon, Lord Pleasance. Did you not? I cannot imagine why."

Lord Pleasance chuckled as Frederick grinned, fully aware that this was the first time that he had stepped out into the fashionable hour ever since he had come to London.

"What was it that brought you here?" Lord Pleasance asked as Frederick let his gaze move around the park and take in the seemingly hundreds of people who had decided to come to Hyde Park. "You, who dislike great crowds and find it to be much too overwhelming... why then come to the fashionable hour?"

Frederick shrugged.

"Because it is a pleasant day," he said, by way of explanation. "And ever since I received your invitation to the dinner party, I have thought that I ought to make myself known in society a little more." His shoulders lifted and then fell. "I am meant to be enjoying myself, am I not? And perhaps being overly cautious is holding me back a little."

"Mayhap it is." Lord Pleasance chuckled and then slapped Frederick on the back. "Goodness, this will be an exceptionally busy day for you, will it not? You will not only be present in Hyde Park but then you will come to dinner also! That will be a lot of people within your sphere in such a short time."

Frederick shrugged but laughed, aware that his friend's gentle teasing was nothing more than that.

"I am certain that I shall manage." Tipping his head, he lifted one eyebrow. "Might I ask who else is coming to this dinner party? Is there anyone else of consequence?"

"Anyone that you are already acquainted with, you mean?" Lord Pleasance grinned. "Yes, Lord Sheffield is attending, Lord and Lady Jefferies and Lord Gibson. You are acquainted with all of them, yes?"

Frederick nodded, a feeling of relief spiraling through him.

"Yes, I am."

"There are also a few new acquaintances who will be attending," Lord Pleasance continued. "You will not know them, I think, but the introductions can be made this evening."

Nodding, Frederick smiled.

"Very well."

"Ah, but there is one of them now!" Lord Pleasance exclaimed, gesturing to someone behind Frederick. "The family, I mean. Lord and Lady Follet and their daughter."

Frederick turned his head and, much to his astonishment saw none other than Miss Fairley, the lady he had embarrassed recently. She was walking a few steps behind a gentleman, a lady, and another young lady, her head dropping forward and her gaze fixed on the ground rather than looking to either side. Frederick's stomach dropped.

"You see them?" Lord Pleasance smiled as Frederick nodded slowly, silently wondering if he had heard Lord Pleasance correctly. "The daughter, Miss Fairley, has recently become acquainted with my wife and, subsequently, we were all introduced. I think them very pleasant people and–"

"You are aware that they have two daughters, are you not?"

The smile on Lord Pleasance's face fixed in place, his eyes rounding.

"I beg your pardon?"

"They have *two* daughters," Frederick repeated,

emphasizing the number. "There is an elder Miss Fairley and a younger Miss Fairley, though both are out." He searched his friend's expression, seeing the shock mounting there. "I confess that I have never been introduced to Lord and Lady Follet nor their elder daughter, but I am acquainted with the younger." Pausing, he studied his friend's face. "You did not know?"

"I was not introduced to the younger, and they made no mention of her," Lord Pleasance said hurriedly, his eyes flaring wide. "That means that I have one extra person for dinner, does it not?"

Frederick offered him a small smile.

"I believe it does."

"But that..." Lord Pleasance closed his eyes and then blew out a long breath, clearly attempting to calm himself. "I think I must return home. Everything will need to be altered!"

"Should you like me to introduce you to the younger Miss Fairley?" Frederick asked, as his friend nodded. "That way, you will be acquainted with her, at least."

"I do not understand why I was not introduced to her at the time," Lord Pleasure exclaimed, throwing up his hands. "Unless she was dancing or the like?"

Frederick thought about this but then shook his head and shrugged. He did not want to tell Lord Pleasance that the young lady was a wallflower, for that would bring her shame and embarrassment and she had already endured enough of that. No, he decided, he would say nothing and hope that Lord Pleasance would not ask any further questions on the matter. At the same time, a needle of concern pressed into his heart. Why would her parents not even think to introduce her? Yes, he knew that she had been a little clumsy with Lord Gibson, but that surely could not be enough of a reason to reject her? His heart squeezed and his brow furrowed as he thought of what she would think when she realized that her parents had accepted a dinner invitation from a new acquaintance and had not thought to introduce her to him.

Mayhap she knows of it already, Frederick thought to himself. *All the same, I must introduce Lord Pleasance to her. It would only be right.*

"Shall we?" Gesturing to the young lady, he saw Lord Pleasance nod, and together, they made their way across the park towards her. Much to Frederick's relief, neither her mother nor father turned to look back at them, leaving the path open for them to speak only to Miss Fairley. Frederick saw the moment when she glanced at them, the moment she recognized his face, given the way that her eyes flared, but, at the very next moment, she looked away again, clearly not expecting them to be at all interested in her.

"Miss Fairley!" Frederick called, making her look at him again. "Might you pause for a moment?"

She did come to a stop, though she glanced at her father and mother who had also stopped to converse with a new acquaintance, their elder daughter standing with them.

"You wish to speak with me?"

Frederick nodded.

"Yes, of course. I have a gentleman I wish to introduce you to."

At this, Miss Fairley's eyes flared, and she took a small step back.

"I beg your pardon?"

"Lord Pleasance," Frederick said quickly, understanding her confusion. "I believe you are to go to dinner with him this evening? He told me that he is not yet acquainted with you, and I wanted very much to make the introduction before the evening came."

Miss Fairley blinked rapidly. Her face went very white indeed.

"Dinner," she said, eventually, her voice cracking. "This evening. Yes, of course." Her smile did not quite reach her eyes and she turned to Lord Pleasance who was smiling warmly. "Yes, Lord Pleasance. How very good to make your acquaintance."

"The pleasure is mine." Lord Pleasance bowed low, doffing his hat. "I must apologize for not pursuing an introduction to you when I first met your parents and your sister. No doubt you would have been dancing at the time, though had I known of your presence, I would have lingered there until your return."

A spot of red came into each of Miss Fairley's cheeks as she looked away, her smile still present but rather faint.

"How very kind," she murmured, neither agreeing, nor disagreeing, with Lord Pleasance's statement.

"You shall have to wait until this evening to be introduced to my wife, unfortunately," Lord Pleasance continued, making Miss Fairley look back at him quickly. "She decided to remain at home this afternoon so she might prepare a little more."

Frederick cleared his throat and Miss Fairley looked at him.

"I shall also be there this evening." When Miss Fairley's eyes flickered, he gestured to Lord Pleasance. "For dinner, I mean."

"Oh." Miss Fairley nodded but then pulled her gaze from Frederick and back to Lord Pleasance. "I shall know someone there then, at least."

"Yes, you shall!" Lord Pleasance exclaimed, sounding quite delighted that he had now been able to make an introduction to the lady. "I think that it shall be a very enjoyable evening, Miss Fairley. I am very glad indeed to be introduced to you at last."

Before Frederick could say more, he caught Lord and Lady Follet turning back towards their daughter. There was mounting surprise on the face of the lady, but Frederick decided that he would take his leave before he was given an introduction to Lord and Lady Follet. At the present moment, he was not particularly enamored of either of them, even though they were not yet introduced. To his mind, they had deliberately left out their younger daughter from the introductions to Lord Pleasance, and that was, Frederick was sure, painful to Miss Fairley – and it was not something which he thought well of either. "I shall leave you now," he said, inclining his head towards Miss Fairley and then to Lord Pleasance. "Until this evening."

"Until this evening," Lord Pleasance replied, though Miss Fairley said nothing.

Instead, her eyes held his for a long moment until Frederick turned away, making him wonder at all that was going on in her mind. Taking in a deep breath, he released it slowly, set his shoulders, and continued to walk across the park.

It *had* been good for him to come out to the fashionable hour this evening, he considered, for it had aided Miss Fairley and that was something he had been glad to do. All the same, Frederick found himself wondering if he would have an opportunity to speak to her this evening and, if that opportunity came, exactly what it was that she would say.

CHAPTER SEVEN

"Lord Pleasance, good afternoon!"

Emma watched as her mother bobbed a quick curtsey, all too aware of how Lady Follet's eyes darted towards her and then away again. Clearly, she was rather confused about why Emma had been speaking to this gentleman, though Emma herself was rather upset at hearing about a dinner invitation that she had no knowledge of. From what Lord Pleasance had said, it seemed as though her mother and father had decided to keep this from her, had chosen only to introduce Martha to him, rather than making any effort to include her also. Thus far, she did not know of any dinner invitation. Was that something her parents had kept hidden from her? Did only *they* wish to attend... but if that was the case, did they expect her simply to remain at home without question or concern?

"Good afternoon, Lady Follet, Lord Follet." Lord Pleasance inclined his head, then gestured to Emma. "I was just now speaking to your younger daughter! I did not know that you were blessed with two daughters, and I am dreadfully sorry that we were not introduced when we first met."

Lady Follet looked at Emma, and then back to Lord Pleasance, and Emma could almost see the way the thoughts were whirling around and around in her mind. No doubt she was wondering whether or not Lord Pleasance was being entirely truthful in terms of his apology, or wondering why they had thought not to introduce her to him.

"There is nothing for you to apologize for, Lord Pleasance!" she said, after a pause of a few moments. "It could not be helped. At the time, my younger daughter was not able to be with us."

"I quite understand," Lord Pleasance replied, smiling. "My wife will be very glad to make her acquaintance also this evening. I look forward to seeing all of you again, there. Good afternoon!"

With that, he touched his hat and then turned on his heel, moving away from them quickly and leaving Emma and her parents alone together.

An ache began to form in Emma's throat as she lifted her chin and looked at her mother steadily. Lady Follet's eyes sharpened for a moment, only for her to then look away again, turning to Lord Follet as though he were the one required to speak next.

"Dinner?" Emma flung out her hands either side, the ache in her throat turning to anger. "You did not tell me that we were to go to join Lord Pleasance and Lady Pleasance for dinner this evening."

Lord Follet cleared his throat.

"Did we not?" His smile was brief. "Well, it is just as well that Lord Pleasance saw you this afternoon. His wife is also quite lovely, and I am sure–"

"You were not going to take me, were you?" Tears began to burn, but Emma blinked them away furiously. "Is that not so?"

Her parents looked at each other again.

"You were not introduced to him, so it did not seem reasonable to expect the invitation to dinner to include you, Emma," her father said, in what sounded like a placating tone. "Surely you can understand that?"

Emma shook her head.

"No, for neither you nor Mama made any attempt to inform Lord Pleasance that I was present at the ball also! You did not even mention my name!" Her hands curled into fists as she looked at her mother and then her father, seeing how they had nothing to say in response, how their eyes met, but no excuse could be given to her. "I am well aware that I am a wallflower, Mama, but that does not mean that I should be ignored, does it? Yes, I can stand at the back of the room at larger social occasions, but when there are invitations for dinner, why should you *want* me to be forgotten? Why should you want me to be left at home?"

"Because," Lady Follet said with a sigh, as though Emma ought to understand without her even needing to ask, "what would happen if you should put your elbow in the soup? What if you should trip and fall into the tea tray? We cannot have any such thing as that, Emma, and therefore it is best if–"

"I am not as ungainly as you believe!" Emma cried,

heedless to those around her. "You do not believe me when I tell you that such incidents have not always been my fault. You are already determined that I am the failure, that I am solely responsible, and you cannot know how much that pains me!"

Without waiting for her mother to respond, Emma turned away and hurried across the park, fully aware that she ought not to be walking by herself while, at the same time, she was desperate to remove herself from her parents and their unfair condemnation. Her heart was torn, broken by their thoughtlessness, and as she walked, tears began to form in the corners of her eyes and she blinked furiously, walking rather blindly as she sought out somewhere quiet to stand. Coming under the shade of a large tree, she leaned back against the trunk, closed her eyes, and dropped her head, taking in long, slow breaths in an attempt to steady herself.

"Miss Fairley?"

Her head lifted sharply, only for her to push herself away from the tree, as she took a few steps back.

"Lord Yeatman, do excuse me. I did not mean to impose myself upon your solitude."

"You did not." He smiled though there was a little sympathy shining in his eyes. "You will find that I am very much inclined towards my own company on many an occasion, Miss Fairley. This is no exception."

She managed a brief smile and then turned her head away.

"I should take my leave again."

Her heart sank as she saw her parents laughing with another lady and gentleman, clearly very well able to set aside all that Emma had said to them. The thought of returning to them so soon was not a pleasant one.

"I do apologize if I have caused you any upset," Lord Yeatman said quietly, coming around to face her again. "It was not my intention. I thought only to introduce Lord Pleasance to you."

Giving him a nod, Emma kept her gaze away from him for fear that he would see her red-rimmed eyes.

"It was appreciated."

"But it did upset you." With a sniff, Emma lifted her chin and then turned her head so that she could not even see Lord Yeatman. The tightness in her throat returned, her eyes were stinging and the sorrow within her was growing with such strength, she could barely catch her breath. "I am sorry for that."

"It was not your doing," she managed to say through trembling lips. "And I am going to be at the dinner this evening after all. That is a good thing."

Much to her surprise, his hand caught hers for a moment and then released it, making her turn back towards him sharply.

"I mean only to offer you a little comfort," he said, a kindness in his eyes which was both wonderful and unexpected. "I understand that this must have been a very difficult situation. I, however, am glad that you will be present at dinner this evening."

She blinked quickly to push the tears back and found her heart leaping, suddenly free of the deep amount of sorrow that had pinned it down. She did not know Lord Yeatman at all, and he might very well be a rogue or a scoundrel, saying those things to her which might then be used to cajole her into a closer acquaintance with him. But as she looked into his light blue eyes, the steadiness there and the way that the edge of his lips curved upwards, she found herself doubting that he could be a rogue.

"That is a nice thing to hear," she said, managing to smile. "You will be, perhaps, the only one who will be glad I am present."

Lord Yeatman tilted his head.

"Why should you say such a thing?"

"Because it is quite true," she said, wondering why she was speaking so truthfully to this gentleman whom she did not know in the least. "My parents have decided that I must be a wallflower – a fact which you already know. In case you are unaware, however, a wallflower is usually ignored and forgotten and that is what is happening to me at present, despite the fact that I have done nothing wrong. Although," she continued, recalling all that Miss Bosworth had stated, and how they had walked through the ballroom as though they were just as any other young lady present, "I am attempting not to let that harm me. I am doing my best to prove to society that I will not let them ignore me."

"That is good." Lord Yeatman made to say more, only to seem to think better of it as he shook his head. "I should take my leave of you now, Miss Fairley. I do not want to damage your reputation."

She looked back at him.

"You are very considerate. Do you not wish to go and speak with others?" Gesturing to the large group of people around them, she lifted one shoulder. "I am sure that there will be many ladies and gentlemen who would wish to be in your company, Lord Yeatman."

"As I have said, I am not always inclined towards company," came the reply as he winced. "I am afraid that it is not something that I always seek out, though I did come here this afternoon so that I might find myself a little happier rather than being unimpressed by my own company!" With a quiet laugh, he inclined his head and then tipped his hat. "Good afternoon, Miss Fairley. I look forward to continuing our conversation this evening."

Emma watched him go, surprised at just how much happier she now felt, after only the smallest of conversations with the gentleman. It was not as though all of her worries and upset had evaporated, simply by being in his company, but it was the kindness of his words and the gentleness of his expression which had soothed her pain a little. Considering him as he walked away, Emma took in his broad shoulders and long back, seeing how he kept his head high as he walked. It was rather surprising to her that such a gentleman was disinclined towards company and, indeed, she had not been sure that he had been speaking the truth, but now, as she let her thoughts turn to him again, and all they had shared, Emma found herself trusting every word.

"I shall have someone to speak with this evening," she murmured to herself, clasping her hands behind her back, and beginning to make her way back to her parents. "That is a good thing."

Even though the pain of her mother and father's disinterest continued to linger, Emma did not feel the same heaviness there any longer. This evening, she *would* go to dinner along with her mother, father, and sister and she *would* have someone eager to speak with her. Acknowledging that, a smile came to her face and, even though her parents barely glanced at her, Emma kept her chin lifted and the smile pinned to her face.

There was *some* joy in this moment, and she would take hold of it with everything she had. After all, she was meant to be trying to force society to take notice of her, was meant to be pushing aside the title of wallflower which the *ton* had decided to attach to her, and this evening would be one way for her to do that.

CHAPTER EIGHT

*L*ord Pleasance shook Frederick's hand firmly.

"Thank you again for the introduction to the younger Miss Fairley this afternoon, my friend."

"But of course," Frederick replied with a smile as Lady Pleasance nodded in agreement. "I am glad that she is able to attend now, with her family."

"As am I. I did not even know that she existed!" Lady Pleasance said as she glanced at her husband. "It was rather odd that she was not introduced, and that her parents did not make mention of her."

Lord Pleasance's expression grew dark for a moment.

"I have been considering that, my dear, and it seems to me that her parents were quite contented to leave her presence unknown, which I do not like."

Frederick winced, his thoughts much in agreement.

"Yes, I would agree that this was what they intended to do. You may not know this, but the younger Miss

Fairley has been pushed into being a wallflower." Keeping his voice low, he glanced around the room, not wanting any of the other guests to overhear him. "I will not go into details, but needless to say, she is rather distressed that such a thing has taken place. I believe that this incident upset her further."

"Then I am all the more grateful to you for your introduction to the lady," Lady Pleasance exclaimed, though she closed her eyes for a moment and thereafter, kept her voice a little lower. "How dreadful that one's parents would deliberately ignore one. I cannot imagine the pain."

"There does not seem to be any reason for her to be a wallflower," Lord Pleasance remarked, rubbing one hand over his chin. "Unless there is some scandal which we are unaware of?"

Frederick shook his head.

"I do not think that there is." Remembering the deep pain which had evidenced itself both in her eyes and in her expression, which had caught at him, he frowned. "She stated that she had done nothing wrong."

"Many a young lady could say that, though I am only playing the devil's advocate with my statements," Lady Pleasance said, quietly. "I am much more inclined to believe the lady's words, given how much she has endured."

Smiling briefly, Frederick spread out his hands on either side.

"I am sure that we would have heard of a scandal, had there been something significant. What she said to me – speaking rather truthfully, I might add – was that her parents had decided that she was to be a wallflower. That does not speak of scandal."

"It might not be a scandal, but it might be something significant," Lady Pleasance said, frowning, "and it might explain why she has been ignored by her parents. Though," she continued, looking at her husband, "now that I have said it, I am sure that something would have been said before now. I am not one inclined towards listening to gossip, though it comes to me regardless! I am sure that I would have heard something by now."

Frederick nodded quickly.

"I shall discover the truth," he found himself saying. "I did say to Miss Fairley that I would look forward to continuing our conversation this evening."

"I should like to be her ally," Lady Pleasance said, reaching out one hand to catch Frederick so that he could not leave without hearing her. "The questions and suggestions I have spoken just now are only intended to challenge our thinking, though I do very much hope that there is nothing untoward there."

"I quite understand and, of course, should she give me permission, then I shall be glad to tell you," Frederick promised. "But I shall go and find the lady now and take my opportunity to speak with her."

"Capital." Lord Pleasance smiled, only to pause as his wife leaned closer, murmuring something in his ear. That smile grew as Frederick watched, seeing his friend nod and then reach to pat his wife's hand. "An excellent suggestion," he said, softly, before looking back to Frederick. "Do not let us hold you back, my friend. Go. Speak with Miss Fairley and let us hope that you soon find the truth."

∼

"Oh." Frederick blinked, then smiled to himself as he stood behind his chair at the dining table, realizing now what Lady Pleasance had whispered into the ear of Lord Pleasance. He was to be seated beside Miss Fairley and that, he was sure, had not been the intention when he had first set foot into Lord Pleasance's house. His smile grew as Miss Fairley glanced at him, though her expression was still rather reserved.

"Good evening, Miss Fairley," he said, seeing her glance at him again. "How excellent it is to be seated with you this evening." Her eyebrows lifted. "I do mean it," he said, waiting until everyone had gathered at the table before assisting her with her chair as she sat, and then taking his seat himself. "You have told me quite plainly that you are a wallflower, Miss Fairley, but that does not mean that I shall treat you as one."

Her eyes flared.

"You do not know me, Lord Yeatman."

"And yet I think it quite unfair for society to treat young ladies in a particular fashion simply because they have been told that they must stay at the side of the room for some inexplicable or unknowable reason."

"Goodness, Lord Yeatman," came the reply, as the soup was served. "There are very few gentlemen who would speak in such a way. I think that you will find yourself in the minority there."

"But did you not tell me that you are doing what you can to force society to recognize you?" The conversation flowed around them without anyone making any sort of attempt to speak to Miss Fairley. That was to their advantage, he considered, for no other guest would be inclined to listen to their conversation or seek to interrupt it – though it was not something that Miss Fairley herself would appreciate, he was sure. She nodded, turning her attention to the soup though she continued to glance at him. "Have you had any sort of success in that?"

Miss Fairley looked at him again.

"We have only just begun, though from our first endeavors, it has not been at all positive." Her eyes darted away again, her shoulders rounding a little. "Most looked at us with disgust or astonishment and no one looked at all pleased."

"But were *you* pleased?"

This time when she looked at him, there was a small smile on her lips which pushed up either side – but only a little.

"I found myself pleased that we were doing something, yes," she agreed, still speaking quietly. "It was Miss Bosworth's influence, for she was the one who stated that she did not want to do as society expected. It was because of her that we stepped out as we did."

"I am sure that your confidence will grow, the more that you do so," Frederick replied, finding himself warming to the lady a good deal. "It must seem very difficult at the present moment, but there will be those in society who will be interested in your company, I am sure. Myself included."

Miss Fairley's smile grew.

"You are very kind, Lord Yeatman, though I confess I must wonder why?"

"Why?"

She nodded.

"Why is it that you show such kindness? Every other member of the *ton* is determined to ignore wallflowers and yet, you do not."

Frederick considered, finding a slight flush of heat creeping up his neck and into his face. What was he to say? That, for whatever reason, she had caught his attention and the situation she found herself in had filled him with sympathy?

"It is because of our chance meeting, Miss Fairley, that is all," he said, realizing that this was not a very clear answer to her question. "As I have told you, I am not one who is inclined towards company very often. I am very careful as to my friends and acquaintances, though I believe that I have been a little *too* cautious of late! After our meeting, I found myself wondering about wallflowers and what it was that placed them there... and realizing what had happened to you, as regards this very dinner, I found myself desirous to show you a little kindness, Miss Fairley, that is all."

Wondering if he had said too much, given the way her cheeks flushed, Frederick turned his attention to his soup and began to eat, realizing too late that almost every other guest had finished their first course and that he had not even brought a spoonful to his mouth. He ate in silence and Miss Fairley said nothing, setting her spoon down and then placing her hands in her lap, waiting for the other guests to be finished.

The soup plates were removed, the second course was served and still, Miss Fairley said nothing. Frederick's heart began to beat a little more quickly, his face now rather hot as he fought to know what he ought to say next. Miss Fairley had not asked him any more questions, nor had she responded to his statement, and now there was a growing tension and awkwardness that he could not seem to fight free from. Swallowing hard, he pressed his lips together and glanced at her again, only to see her catch his eye.

"That is appreciated, Lord Yeatman." Miss Fairley finally smiled, though her hazel eyes swirled with something that he could not quite make out. "It is very difficult being a wallflower when one has done nothing to deserve such censure. To have – oh!"

At the very moment she spoke, the footman who was serving the second course to her, seemed to sway or stumble, for the plate half-fell, half-dropped onto the table, and sent the cutlery rattling. The meat that the host had carved and then placed onto Miss Fairley's plate sent its juices splattering across the table and then onto the table, making every other guest turn to look at Miss Fairley.

"Oh, I am so dreadfully sorry!" Before Frederick knew what he was doing, he had risen to his feet and then handed Miss Fairley his napkin. "I should not have gesticulated so wildly! My deepest apologies." Lifting his gaze, he looked at every other guest in turn, catching the way that Lord and Lady Follet frowned in the direction of their daughter. "I am terribly sorry, Lord Pleasance. I did not mean to interrupt nor cause this dreadful situation."

"It is quite all right."

Lord Pleasance gave him a nod and Frederick, hoping that his friend could understand that there was something more to this situation, nodded back before taking his seat. The footman was deeply apologetic also, but Lord Pleasance not only reassured him but then spoke to Miss Fairley, who smiled and assured him that she was quite all right. The dinner resumed, the conversation began to flow again and Frederick, letting out a slow breath of relief that he had managed to take the attention away from Miss Fairley, picked up his cutlery to begin the second course.

"You did not have to do that for me, Lord Yeatman."

Frederick looked at her.

"I am aware that I did not, Miss Fairley, but I did not want you to be unnecessarily embarrassed."

She held his gaze for a long moment, clearly considering what he had said and what that meant.

"Your kindness is unsurpassed, Lord Yeatman. I think..." She frowned and then looked away. "There is more to your action than you can know and, for that, I am deeply appreciative."

Not understanding what she meant, but choosing not to question her at that moment, given all that had just taken place, Frederick simply smiled and then returned his attention to the dinner. His smile began to fade away as he let himself consider what had just happened. What had caused the footman to stumble in that way? Miss Fairley had done nothing, for she had not moved nor gestured nor done anything to startle the footman – so why had the plate fallen from his hand in such a way? It was all very strange indeed.

CHAPTER NINE

*E*mma swung her leg idly as she sat in the drawing room, her gaze on the window and the last few wisps of the day's light that made its way through it. It had been a sennight since the dinner party and still, through all that time, she had not forgotten about the incident, nor about Lord Yeatman. He had been exceptionally kind to her in speaking to the rest of the guests as he had done, taking the blame for something that absolutely had not been his fault. That had been an act of kindness far beyond anything she had ever experienced and, whilst she had been to a few occasions since then – though still remaining with her wallflower friends – Emma had not been able to forget about him.

A soft smile lifted the corners of her mouth as she thought about Lord Yeatman's declaration that the spillage had been entirely his own doing. He had been very fervent in his explanation, and she was sure that most of the guests had believed him, even if she *had* caught Lady Pleasance looking at her with a slightly lifted eyebrow, though she had smiled when Emma had caught her gaze. That was something at least.

"Emma?" Lady Follet came into the room, disturbing Emma's peace and giving her a disgruntled look which Emma immediately understood to indicate that she did not want to see her sitting so casually. "Are you quite prepared? Why ever are you sitting so?"

"I am ready for the soiree, yes," Emma said quickly, rising to her feet and smoothing one hand down her skirt. "I have been waiting for my sister to be ready and—"

"I do hope that you have not wrinkled your gown." With a sniff, Lady Follet beckoned for Emma to follow her. "Your sister is waiting at the door and your father is already in the carriage!"

"No one came to fetch me," Emma protested weakly, as her mother shooed her out of the room. "If I had known—"

"Do hurry up," her mother interrupted, firmly. "Now, you know what my expectations are for you this evening, do you not?"

Emma frowned.

"Are they not the same as every other time you have spoken to me?" she asked, her tone dropping a little. "You expect me to stand with my friends. With the other wallflowers."

Lady Follet ushered her up into the carriage and Emma sat down opposite her sister and beside her father, leaving Lady Follet to take the opposite seat. Lord Follet rapped on the roof and the carriage began to move away and, though Emma thought the conversation was at an end, Lady Follet reached across to catch her hand and her attention.

"We are aware of what the other wallflowers have been doing," she said, with more severity in her voice than Emma had expected. "For whatever reason, you have decided to join them and we find that to be most displeasing."

Emma's eyebrows shot towards her hairline.

"I have been doing nothing wrong, Mama. I am only walking with my friends and conversing with them as I please. Just because society demands that we stay at the back of the room does not mean that this is what we *must* do."

Lady Follet released Emma's hand.

"But it is safer for you, there," she protested, as though she were seeking to help Emma. "Your father and I do not like it. It is–"

"I am aware of that, Mama," Emma said clearly, aware that she ought not to be interrupting her mother but finding her heart beginning to quicken with a mixture of upset and a stirring of anger. "I am sure that there are many in society who do not much like to see those that they have designated as wallflowers doing what they believe wallflowers ought not to do." She glanced at her father but he, much to her relief, had his eyes closed and appeared to either be dozing or paying very little attention to what Emma had to say. "My friends and I do not like simply standing at the back of the room, watching what is going on. We have decided, of late, to simply walk and talk together during whatever occasion we have attended. That is not something I intend to give up."

Her mother clicked her tongue and shook her head before looking at her husband. Seeing Lord Follet's closed eyes and clear lack of interest in what was being said, Lady Follet's shoulders slumped, and Emma looked out of the window quickly, trying not to let a slightly triumphant smile spread across her face. It was not as though everything was going well, despite her attempts to step into society with the other wallflowers. It was not as though gentlemen and ladies turned to greet them, that many were eager to become acquainted with them or dance with them. Most continued to glance at them, then look away again, and some had even turned their backs. It was not the same for every wallflower, however. One or two of Emma's friends had enjoyed a little more success, though Emma herself was not one of them.

Though Lord Yeatman has not ignored me, she thought to herself, finding herself smiling at the thought. *I do wonder if I will see him this evening.*

∽

"My mother has shown a little displeasure in our acting like this." Emma sighed and took Miss Simmons' offered arm as they began to make their way around the ballroom. "She has not said it outright, but I think she should like to order me to remain in the shadows."

"I am still a little unsure of why you have been determined as a wallflower," her friend replied, quietly. "For most of us, there is a clear reason – albeit an unfair one in most cases – but for you, there can be nothing said really."

"Might I interrupt?"

Emma turned her head in surprise, only to see Lord Yeatman step a little closer, a broad smile on his face.

"Forgive me for the interruption, but I thought it right for me to greet you both this evening. It is my pleasure to see you again, Miss Simmons, Miss Fairley. Are you finding the ball pleasant entertainment?"

Miss Simmons sighed and shook her head as Lord Yeatman's smile grew sympathetic.

"It is rather dull only watching rather than participating, Lord Yeatman, though I must say that it is certainly better to walk and converse and smile at those around us instead of hiding away in the shadows."

Lord Yeatman's gaze turned to Emma, his eyebrow lifting.

"Ah, I recall that you explained to me that both you and your friends hoped to break free of society's constraints as regards wallflowers. Are you having any success?"

"Some." Emma offered him a smile, finding her heart warming at both his presence and the conversation with the gentleman. "It is trying when most of society rejects your company, I confess."

"Especially when there is no reason for it!" Miss Simmons exclaimed, gesturing to Emma. "I was just saying to Miss Fairley that I can see no reason for *her* to be pushed back in such a way. It is most unfair."

Emma's face flushed hot as she blinked and then glanced at Miss Simmons. Her friend had inadvertently given more away than Emma had desired and thus, she now found herself in something of a predicament. Ought she to explain to Lord Yeatman the reason behind her situation? Or should she remain silent?

"I should be glad to hear it if you would like to share it with me." As if he had read her thoughts, Lord Yeatman smiled but then shrugged. "But I will not press you. If you think it best to keep such thoughts to yourself, then I quite understand."

"Oh, it is for a very foolish reason," Miss Simmons interjected, waving one hand before Emma could speak again. "I am sure that there is nothing to hide."

The decision taken from her, Emma coughed lightly and then caught Miss Simmons' eyes flaring, evidently realizing too late that she had said too much.

"It *is* foolishness, I suppose," Emma agreed, pausing for a moment as she looked to Lord Yeatman. "My mother and father have stated that I am rather inelegant at times, as you are well aware."

Lord Yeatman's eyebrows lifted, his eyes rounding.

"Do you mean to say that such a thing is your only reason for being pressed back into this situation?"

Rather surprised at the gentleman's reaction, Emma nodded slowly.

"Yes, that is so."

"Goodness." Lord Yeatman lifted one hand to his chin, rubbing at it for a moment as his gaze drifted away from her. "How extraordinary."

"Though I must thank you for what you did at the dinner party," Emma said, aware that she had already thanked him, but finding herself compelled to thank him again. "You were most generous. In truth, I do not know what happened, but I can say for certain that it was not *your* doing."

Lord Yeatman looked back at her sharply, his jaw a little tight.

"I can assure you that it was not your doing either, Miss Fairley."

She looked at him and then smiled rather wearily.

"I do not know what happened, as I have said. For whatever reason, however, it appears to me that such accidents follow me. Some are certainly my fault but others..." Aware that she was saying more to him than she had meant, Emma dropped her hands. "It is rather tiring, and I can understand, I suppose, why my parents seek to push me back from society. My sister is also seeking a match and must be considered."

Lord Yeatman made to say something, only to close his mouth again and give a slight shake of his head.

"It is unfortunate that such a consequence has been placed upon Miss Fairley, is it not?" Miss Simmons, whose cheeks had gone rather red, given that she now understood what she had said, offered Emma a small smile and then looked to Lord Yeatman again. "I personally have not seen any ungainliness from Miss Fairley ever since she became my friend."

Lord Yeatman smiled, his expression softening as he took in Miss Simmons' words.

"I am sure that you have not."

"It seems very unfair that the *ton* would ignore her," Miss Simmons continued, making Emma frown at the way her friend was pushing her forward towards Lord Yeatman, though she had never expressed a desire for her to do such a thing. "Though I, personally, believe that it is most unfair for the *ton* to treat us *all* in such a way as this!"

"Please, there is no need–"

"No, you are quite right," Lord Yeatman interrupted, sending Emma a somewhat apologetic smile for interrupting her. "I am quite in agreement with you, Miss Simmons. The *ton* should not be treating you in such a way, especially for such a foolish reason as supposed clumsiness!"

Miss Simmons pressed her lips together.

"Though there is a different reason for my own situation," she said, as Lord Yeatman shrugged. "You should be aware of that."

Lord Yeatman shook his head.

"No, I do not require any explanation, Miss Simmons. What I *do* require, however, are your dance cards, if you would be so willing as to give them to me?"

Emma blinked in surprise, a sudden thrill rushing up her spine as she glanced at Miss Simmons, seeing nothing but sheer joy in her friend's expression.

"You... you wish to dance with us?"

Lord Yeatman nodded.

"Yes, I do. Would you like to step out with me?"

Before Emma could respond, Miss Simmons had practically thrown her dance card to Lord Yeatman, leaving Emma to follow suit. When she handed it to him, the smile on his face sent another rush of delight into her heart and she could not prevent the bright smile which spread across her face as he took it from her. This was the first time that she was to dance with any gentleman in weeks and the thought of being in his arms was a somewhat thrilling one.

her feelings were immediately dampened by the recollection of what had occurred previously when she had danced with other gentlemen. She had tripped and slipped and fallen and knocked into other couples. What if that were to happen again?

"Shall we say the cotillion, Miss Simmons?" Lord Yeatman handed the dance card back to the lady and then looked at Emma. "Do you have any preference, Miss Fairley?"

Emma swallowed tightly, pressing her lips flat for a moment.

"I – I should tell you that the last time I danced with a gentleman, there was something of a commotion thereafter." Recalling that Lord Gibson was friends with Lord Yeatman, Emma closed her eyes for a moment in embarrassment. "Which you are already aware of, I know."

"I have no concerns and certainly no fear," he told her, looking down at her dance card. "The country dance, mayhap? Or the waltz?"

Emma's eyes shot to his.

"The waltz?" The words came out a little strangled, her heart slamming hard into her chest as he nodded. "You wish to dance the waltz with me?"

"Why should I not?"

Miss Simmons caught her breath and Emma, aware of the heat rippling up her face, managed to nod.

"That would be very kind of you, Lord Yeatman. I do not think that I have had opportunity to step out into the waltz as yet."

"Then I shall be delighted to take it." Still smiling, he wrote his initials down on her dance card and then handed it back to her. "I look forward to dancing with you both." With another nod, he stepped back. "I shall permit you to escape my company for a short while, at least. Until later this evening, Miss Simmons, Miss Fairley."

It was in something of a daze that Emma found herself being led forward, barely able to take in what had happened. Miss Simmons was saying something in hushed and excited tones, but Emma could barely hear her. Lord Yeatman was, she knew, a kind gentleman, but taking the waltz from her seemed to be a little more than a kindness. Was there a flicker of interest there? Or was she reading more into this situation than there really was?

"You must be so very excited!"

Emma blinked furiously, trying to steel herself as she looked to Miss Simmons.

"Excited?"

Her friend nodded eagerly.

"The waltz? The waltz with Lord Yeatman? That is wonderful!"

"Any kind of dance is wonderful," Emma replied, doing her utmost not to concentrate on the kind of dance he had chosen for her. "To be given any sort of attention is very generous indeed."

"But the *waltz*!" Miss Simmons exclaimed, pulling Emma closer. "That gentleman might have something of a consideration for you, Emma!"

Sensing a flare of hope rising in her heart, Emma quickly dismissed the idea before it could take root.

"No, I do not believe that," she stated, firmly. "I am not particularly well acquainted with Lord Yeatman as yet, but what I *do* know of him is that he is very generous, considerate, and unwilling to permit society to dictate how he must act. That is all this is. A generous act which is meant only as an encouragement to me."

Miss Simmons tossed her head, though a smile still lingered on her face.

"I believe it is more than that," she said, making Emma smile regardless of her attempts to hide that from her friend. "Just think of it! A waltz with a gentleman! How exciting that is going to be."

"So long as I do not trip and fall," Emma replied, a little ruefully, "or tread on his toes or knock into another couple."

"Nothing like that will take place," Miss Simmons stated without even a second of hesitation. "It is going to be a wonderful dance, I am sure of it."

CHAPTER TEN

The thought of dancing with Miss Fairley had been one thing, but taking her into his arms and sweeping her around the floor had been quite another. Frederick was rather surprised at just how well she danced, given what she had told him. They danced with ease, with the lady following his lead without a single hesitation and a light smile on her face which, Frederick hoped, meant that she was enjoying the dance as much as he was. His breathing a little fast from the dance, Frederick continued to spin her around the floor in time with all of the other couples until the music began to slow, signaling the end of the dance.

With a small smile, Frederick slowed his steps until, finally, they came to a stop. Stepping back from her, Frederick inclined his head into a bow just as Miss Fairley curtsied, though this was done perfectly and without a single wobble or tremble. To his mind, Miss Fairley was not at all ungainly or clumsy. In fact, she had as much poise and elegance as any young lady of his acquaintance! As Miss Fairley rose, she let out such a long breath of relief that Frederick could not help but smile, only for color to flood through her face.

"You are relieved, yes?"

"Yes, I am." Miss Fairley took his arm the moment that it was offered and, much to Frederick's surprise, he felt her trembling just a little. "You cannot know the extent of my nervousness, Lord Yeatman."

"But why should you feel any such thing?" he asked, finding himself rather concerned for the lady. "You have danced many times before, I am sure."

"Yes," she agreed, glancing at him, though her face was still filled with color, "but I have also fallen on some occasions, or stepped on the foot of another."

Frederick chuckled, bringing her back to the gathered crowd who had made space for the dancing, though there was no one there waiting for her, no parent or friend. Miss Simmons had stepped out to dance with another gentleman – much to her delight – though Frederick presumed she would come in search of Miss Fairley thereafter. For the moment, he had the lady all to himself.

"I would be lying if I said that I had not done the same, Miss Fairley."

She smiled then, relief ending the trembling within her frame.

"Though perhaps not with as much frequency, Lord Yeatman?"

"I could not say."

A small sigh escaped her, though the smile remained.

"I have always told my parents that I cannot take responsibility for all that has happened, though I certainly have been willing to accept some of the blame on some occasions. Unfortunately, however, they appear to be quite unwilling to believe that which, in a way, I can understand."

A little confused, Frederick frowned.

"What do you mean?"

"I mean that, if it appears that *I* am the one who is responsible for all of these accidents and mishaps, then why should they not blame me? To them, I am sure that it appears that I am simply doing what I can to make myself appear a little less guilty than they think me to be. Does that make sense?"

Frederick nodded slowly, finding that the swell of sympathy in his heart was growing all the more with every word that came from her mouth. For whatever reason, he found himself believing that she was not entirely responsible for all that had happened in her past, even though he had no real knowledge of everything that had taken place. His mind drifted back to the dinner they had enjoyed some days ago, recalling what had happened with the footman. A frown settled over his features.

"You recall what happened at Lord and Lady Pleasance's dinner as regards the footman?"

Miss Fairley looked at him sharply.

"Yes, of course I do. I did thank you for that and–"

Frederick shook his head no.

"I do not seek any further thanks, Miss Fairley. It is only that I wondered if you had any thoughts on what might have happened on that occasion?"

"With the footman?" When he nodded, Miss Fairley shook her head. "No, I confess that I do not think I do. I am very confused, truth be told, for I do not know what I did to upset his hand from the plate and–"

"I do not think that you did anything." Without meaning to do it, Frederick reached out and took Miss Fairley's hand, grasping it tightly. "I do not think that you did a single thing. And if it is as you say, if you are not responsible for the other things which have happened, then might there not be something there which could suggest that..." Seeing her eyebrows lift, Frederick trailed off, heat burning its way up his chest and into his face. He was saying too much, he realized, speaking without thinking, without truly considering what it was that he wanted to say. He cleared his throat and dropped her hand. "Forgive me."

"No, please." Miss Fairley's eyes fastened to his, unrelenting in their steady gaze. "What was it that you were going to say?"

Frederick hesitated, then shook his head.

"It is nothing. We are not particularly well acquainted as yet; Miss Fairley and I do not want to say anything which would upset you."

She held his gaze and remained silent. Frederick swallowed hard, aware that she was not about to let him say anything more. Whether he wished to or not, he would have to speak the words that had come to him, regardless of whether they were wise or not.

"Very well, though I pray that, if what I say upsets you in any way, you will not hold it against me," he said, with a half-smile as she nodded fervently. "Miss Fairley, I do not know if you have any enemies – I would guess that you do not – but I do wonder if someone is attempting to do these things to you."

Miss Fairley held his gaze steadily for a long time, without saying a single word. Buzzing came into Frederick's ears, and he could barely look into her face, his heart thundering and his mind whispering at him about how foolish he had been. He wanted to break the silence, wanted to say something that would be both an apology and words of regret, but no words came to him. All he could do was stare back at her and wait.

"I see." Miss Fairley began to blink rapidly, then passed one hand over her eyes, making Frederick fear that he had not only managed to upset her, but had also made her cry. "That is... a heavy thought."

"It is a foolish one," Frederick protested, quickly. "It was nothing but nonsense. Perhaps I was being too fervent in my attempts to help you but–"

"It is not foolish." Miss Fairley dropped her hand and gazed back into his eyes. "Lord Yeatman, it is not in the *least* bit foolish. In fact, it is something that would explain a good deal, would it not? It would help me to understand all that has taken place and to make sense of my present situation. If, as you saw, I did nothing to upset the footman at our dinner, then why else did he jerk and drop the plate in such a fashion? And," she continued, her eyes now flaring wide, "if I did *not* knock the tray from the footman's hand when I finished my dance with Lord Gibson, then what caused that footman to drop it?"

"I do not know," Frederick said slowly, a little surprised that she had reacted in such a positive manner. "Then might I ask if you are in agreement with me, Miss

Fairley? You think that there *might* be someone who is attempting to injure you in such a way?"

Miss Fairley paused for a long moment and then, eventually, began to nod.

"Yes, I think that there is certainly the possibility of such a thing."

"Then do you have any thoughts on who it might be?" Frederick stood closer to her, a sudden excitement catching at his heart. "Do you have someone in your life who might wish you ill?"

Immediately, Miss Fairley shook her head and the light in her eyes began to fade.

"No, I do not. In that regard, Lord Yeatman, I am quite at a loss."

"Oh."

"But it is something which I shall have to continue to consider," she added, offering him a small smile. "I do value your thoughts in that regard, Lord Yeatman. I would never have thought of such an idea myself."

"I can help you."

Frederick watched as Miss Fairley blinked and then frowned. Her face no longer held any hint of color, and he quickly began to realize just how much his words had upset her. None of her problems were his doing, of course, for he was not the one upsetting her in that regard but clearly, the suggestion itself had set her awry.

"I think that you have done enough when it comes to assisting me, Lord Yeatman." Miss Fairley reached out and touched his hand and, as she did so, fire swept right up his arm. "You have already taken the blame at that dinner party, and now you have not only danced with me

– a wallflower – but given me a clear suggestion of what might truly be happening in my present circumstances. I do not know what I am to do next but–"

"I have an idea." The idea took hold of him with such fierceness, he could barely catch his breath. "You have already told me that the wallflowers – you and your friends, I mean – are to go about in society just as usual. You are attempting to step away from the confines placed upon you by society and, in doing so, seek instead to force society to take note of you. Therefore, would it not be more likely that what has happened to you in the past as regards your... mishaps, might they not be more likely to continue?"

Miss Fairley's eyebrows lifted high, her eyes rounding.

"Miss Simmons did say that she thought it odd that there were no such mishaps or the like during the time I have been a wallflower, hiding away in the shadows."

"Which gives my thoughts all the more credence, does it not?" Frederick did not say such a thing with any hint of arrogance, but rather the understanding that what Miss Simmons had said fitted in with the suggestion that there was someone else behind this. "If you have been pushed to the back of the room, then you are no longer visible. You are no longer present in society, are you? So perhaps in that way, this person has gained what they wanted... though I presume you do not know why that would be?"

Miss Fairley shook her head.

"No, not in the least. I have very few friends – though more now that I have become a wallflower – and there is no reason for any of them to try to remove me from my situation. My sister is often in the company of one Lord Wellbridge, and there is every hope of a match there, so I cannot see who would do such a thing, *or* understand why they might behave so."

Frederick nodded slowly.

"Then let me be of assistance to you," he said, seeing her smile gently. "If you are to be in society again, if you are to be in company and the like, then I can be often with you. I can watch from a distance, take note of who is around you and who might be seeking to injure you."

Miss Fairley's expression softened.

"You would be willing to do that for me?"

Frederick nodded.

"But of course."

"Why?" The question hung in the air between them, and Frederick found himself struggling for an answer. He could not quite explain what it was about Miss Fairley's situation that had him so fervent in his desire to aid her and in that, he could not find an answer to give her. Instead, he simply lifted his shoulders and smiled. "You are simply kindness itself, though you are too good to say," Miss Fairley told him, putting one hand to her heart as her eyes grew a little glassy. "I do not think that I have ever had anyone express such generosity to me, Lord Yeatman – save for my friends, of course. The other wallflowers accepted me, pulled me to them, and comforted me in my difficulty and I will always be grateful to them for that. They are as I am and in that, the sweetness of their friendship is something I will always be thankful for. However, when it comes to you, there is no reason for you to be of aid to me. I have done nothing which would encourage you to be a support to me and yet, your kind heart can do nothing other than be willing to do so." She swallowed and blinked quickly again, her hand falling to her side. "You cannot know how grateful I am to you for that."

"I do not mean to upset you."

She laughed then, albeit a little brokenly as she shook her head, her copper curls bouncing lightly.

"No, you have not, Lord Yeatman. I am not in the least bit upset. I am overwhelmed, certainly, and there is much for me to think on, but upset, I am not." Reaching out, she touched his hand again and that same fire ran up his arm though he fought to hide the shock of that touch from his expression. The softness in her hazel eyes, the sweetness of her smile, and the sheer joy in her expression caught hold of him, and he could not look away. "Thank you," she said, quietly. "Thank you for your kindness. It means more to me than I can ever express."

CHAPTER ELEVEN

"There is something I should like to tell you all."
Looking around at the small group of her gathered friends, Emma took a deep breath and tried to settle herself before she spoke further. It had been two days since Lord Yeatman had spoken with her about his thoughts regarding her present situation and, since that time, she had barely been able to think of anything else. "I do hope that you will indulge me for a few minutes?"

Her friends all nodded, though one or two glanced at each other, clearly a little concerned about what Emma might say.

"I am not about to renege on our decision to go about society as we have been doing," Emma said quickly, seeing the worry in Miss Bosworth's expression. "It is, in fact, to do with my situation and the concerns that have come with it."

"What do you mean?" Lady Alice asked, coming to stand a little closer as the soiree continued all around them. "What about your situation is concerning?"

Emma glanced around the drawing room, but no one was looking in their direction. That was to be expected, she supposed, but all the same, she wanted to be quite certain that no one would overhear her words.

"It is something that Miss Simmons said to me," she began, smiling at her friend, who immediately looked rather surprised. "You stated that there had been no upsets or the like ever since I had been forced to become a wallflower."

Clearly remembering this, Miss Simmons nodded fervently.

"Yes, I recall saying that to you. That is why you were asked to stand back, was it not? Because of all the many mishaps that supposedly were caused by your ungainliness."

Emma nodded, her face flushing a little as one or two incidents came back to her mind.

"Yes, that is so."

"But nothing like that has happened since you became a wallflower?" Lady Frederica frowned, though Emma nodded, confirming that this was true. "That does not make very much sense."

"Which is exactly what I said," Miss Simmons added, almost triumphantly. "Though why such a thing should be true, I do not know."

"Nor did I," Emma replied, looking around at the small group. "Though Lord Yeatman has made a suggestion which has given me pause."

"Lord Yeatman?" Miss Bosworth smiled suddenly. "He is a kind gentleman, I think. Ever since he has become acquainted with you, Miss Fairley, he has always sought us out and greeted us at any ball or soiree we have attended. He clearly does not want to react in the same way as the rest of society."

"And that is by design," Emma agreed, smiling. "He does not want to treat us as the rest of society do. Therefore, he danced not only with me but also with Miss Simmons recently and it was after this waltz that he spoke to me about his thoughts on my present situation."

Lady Alice and Lady Frederica exchanged a glance, though Emma did her best not to consider it too much. There was little point in wondering what her friends thought of Lord Yeatman's consideration of her, not when she had so much to say.

"What are his thoughts?" Miss Simmonds wanted to know. "Does he think you are in danger?"

Emma shook her head.

"No, not in that regard. Do you recall what I told you about the dinner I attended some days ago?" Seeing all her friends nod, Emma gave them a small smile. "Lord Yeatman took the blame so that it would not be placed upon me. Upon hearing what Miss Simmons had said, and upon considering himself what had happened at the dinner, Lord Yeatman stated that he thought there might be someone attempting to injure me in some way. Not that I would be in any physical danger, but rather that these things are being put upon *my* shoulders when, in fact, they were the deliberate action of someone else."

Her friends all looked rather astonished, though Miss Simmons was the first to speak.

"That would make sense, given that no such happenings have taken place since you joined us," she said quickly, unwittingly agreeing with Lord Yeatman's considerations. "You were forced to become a wallflower. Therefore, there was no need for this person to do as they had been, if their aim was to keep you away from society."

Emma spread out her hands, lifting her shoulders as she did so.

"Mayhap. That is Lord Yeatman's consideration."

"Goodness!" Lady Frederica looked a little alarmed, her eyes wide. "But for what cause? Why would someone wish you to be pushed from society? What is it that you have done that would bring about such disfavor?"

Emma's skin prickled but she forced a smile.

"I have done nothing," she said, seeing the way that Lady Frederica's cheeks flooded with heat. "That is what is most peculiar. There is nothing that I have done – or that I can recall having done – that would cause anyone to become angry with me. So why then would someone wish for society to turn its back upon me?"

Silence fell upon the group, only for Miss Simmons to sigh aloud.

"If you do not know, Miss Fairley, then certainly none of us can surmise!"

"Indeed." Emma leaned a little closer, keeping her voice low. "But Lord Yeatman has suggested that he can be of aid to me, though no one can be allowed to become aware of his true purpose. Given that we are all now moving about society as we please – albeit with chagrin from various members of the *ton,* he feels that this person, whoever they are, might continue with such attacks. Therefore, he has said that he will watch our interactions, and will take care to note any unusual occurrences which might take place without my awareness."

"That is very good of him," Miss Simmons murmured, though her expression was a little troubled. "That is a little worrying though, is it not? You have someone who is seeking to harm your reputation in society without having any understanding of why they might be doing so... and even who they might be!"

Emma gave her friend a small, wry smile.

"Yes, it is rather troubling," she agreed, quietly, "but in truth, I do feel a little relief in this. I have always told my parents that I have not been fully responsible for all that has taken place and, though they have not accepted that, if what Lord Yeatman believes is true, then I will have evidence – proof, even – that I have been right all along."

Her friends all looked at each other but, much to Emma's relief, all of them appeared to be quite willing to support her, given the nods and the smiles on some of their faces.

"Then you can have my support in this also, of course," Miss Simmons agreed, quietly. "I do not know what it is that I can do, but anything that will be of use, I will willingly offer it."

"I thank you."

"I will do whatever I can to be of aid to you as well," Lady Alice chimed in, as did Lady Frederica and Miss Bosworth. "This does sound both mysterious and rather disconcerting, I must say. I do find myself a little troubled on your behalf."

Emma clasped her hands tightly in front of her, her

heart beginning to beat a little more quickly as she considered all that her friends had said. She would be a fool to say that she had no qualms about her present situation. Yes, there was relief to think that she was going to be able to prove that she was not fully responsible for all that had taken place but, at the same time, there was also worry and concern about who was behind it all... and what it was that they wanted from her.

"Thank you all. I am a little worried, I will admit, but there is nothing to be gained from that. I must strike forward, I must continue as we have begun, in the hope that I will find the truth, and perhaps be able to return to society."

Lady Frederica smiled.

"That is what we all hope for, is it not," she said, a small sigh escaping her. "Let us hope that this Lord Yeatman of yours can bring you some answers."

A fire immediately lit Emma's cheeks as she fought the urge to press her hands to them.

"Lord Yeatman is a gentleman with exceptional kindness, that is all," she said, firmly. "I will be forever grateful to him for his generosity and his willingness to behave as many others would not. It says a great deal about his character, I think." With a smile, she spread out her hands again and then let them fall. "Let us hope that we *all* will find our way back into society, one way or another. That this Season will be our last as wallflowers of London society!"

"A calling card, my Lady."

Lady Follet yawned and took it from the butler, though her expression became rather puzzled.

"A Viscount Yeatman?"

Emma's head shot up as the butler nodded and was then sent by her mother to bring Lord Yeatman into the drawing room. Thus far, it had been only her sister who had received gentlemen for, though these fellows greeted them both and spoke well to them, it was quite obvious that their only interest was in Martha. That was to be expected, Emma had reasoned, for the gentlemen would not know her and therefore, their interest would be turned to Martha. Thus, Emma had sat quietly, drunk rather too many cups of tea and had done her best to appear bright-eyed and paying full attention, though the last gentleman – Lord Kinston – had been something of a bore and Emma had noticed even her mother's eyes drooping at one point.

Lord Yeatman, however, had clearly come to call upon *her*, for he was not yet acquainted with Martha.

"Who?" Lady Follet rose from her chair and looked to Martha rather than to Emma. "Do you know this gentleman?"

"Lord Yeatman?" Martha shook her head. "No, I–"

"You were introduced at Lord Pleasance's dinner," Emma interrupted, aware that the door could open at any moment to permit Lord Yeatman entry. "He was seated next to me."

Her sister's eyes widened suddenly.

"Oh, he caused that slight embarrassment with the footman at the dinner table, did he not?"

Emma nodded but could say nothing more, for the door opened and Lord Yeatman was presented, though he was swiftly followed by another gentleman – one Emma recognized immediately as Lord Wellbridge. Martha's expression drew up into a state of happiness as she greeted both gentlemen, though Emma chose to say nothing, curtseying only instead.

"How very pleasant to have *two* gentlemen calling at once!" Lady Follet exclaimed as Lord Wellbridge and Lord Yeatman sat down. "The tea tray will arrive momentarily. I presume that you are acquainted with each other?"

Lord Yeatman nodded, though, much to Emma's surprise, Lord Wellbridge frowned – whether that was due to his lack of recognition or for some other reason, she could not say.

"We are, though it was some time ago," Lord Yeatman explained, his words bringing a lightness to Lord Wellbridge's expression. "It was before my father passed away. My title, at that time, was Galson." He chuckled as a look of clear understanding passed across Lord Wellbridge's face. "You recall me now, I see."

"Yes, I do indeed! That *was* some years ago," Lord Wellbridge exclaimed, just as the tea tray was brought in. "How very good to be in your company again. Might I ask how you are acquainted with this very fine family?"

Emma watched as Martha went to pour the tea, noticing with some concern how her sister's hand trembled a little, though, no doubt, that came from her desire to please Lord Wellbridge and perhaps, from her delight in being in his company.

"I was first acquainted with Miss Emma Fairley," Lord Yeatman said, a smile in his voice as Emma caught his eye, aware of the sudden flare of warmth in her chest as she returned his smile with one of her own. "Thereafter, it was through Lord Pleasance's dinner that we all became acquainted, was it not?"

Lady Follet nodded, though her eyes sharpened as she looked at Emma, perhaps having never understood that Emma had been previously acquainted with the gentleman.

"Yes, that is quite so. The dinner was marvelous, was it not?"

Lord Yeatman chuckled again.

"I suppose it was, though I will say that my mishap at the dining table did make for a little embarrassment!"

"Oh, but I am sure that it has all been forgotten!" Lady Follet laughed as Emma did her best not to roll her eyes and picked up her tea instead. "We shall have to enjoy another dinner with you, Lord Yeatman, to prove that nothing untoward will happen should you sit to dine with company again."

Lord Yeatman laughed at this, though his gaze went quickly back to Emma, leaving her suddenly a little breathless. There was no space for quiet conversation here, no opportunity for them to speak privately at length so why, then, had he come to call?

"I wonder, Miss Fairley, if you should like to take a walk with me in the park tomorrow?"

Emma blinked, her silent question suddenly answered as Lord Yeatman smiled at her, his blue eyes alight with what appeared to be hope.

"Lord Yeatman, I—"

"I presume you are speaking to my elder daughter?" Lady Follet interrupted Emma before she could finish speaking and instantly, Emma's face flamed as she dropped her head, unable to look at anyone else in the room. "Miss *Martha* Fairley?"

There was a slight pause, only for Lord Yeatman to clear his throat.

"No, Lady Follet, though I mean no slight nor disrespect. I was, in fact, speaking to your younger daughter, Miss Emma."

Carefully, Emma peeked at her mother from under her lashes, seeing her mother's eyes flared wide for a moment, her mouth forming a perfect circle.

"Miss Fairley?" Lord Yeatman continued when Lady Follet did not respond. "What say you? Tomorrow? Or the day after that if you are already engaged in another activity tomorrow."

Emma swallowed and then nodded, a sudden buzzing in her ears, her heart thumping furiously.

"I am not engaged in any activity tomorrow, Lord Yeatman."

He grinned at her.

"Then should you like to walk with me? Perhaps in St James' Park? I always find Hyde Park a little too busy."

Remembering what he had confessed to her about being a little overwhelmed by too many gentlemen and ladies in one space, Emma managed to smile.

"Yes, of course. St James' Park."

"Excellent." Lord Yeatman nodded and then rose to his feet. "I shall not take up any more of your time. I look forward to tomorrow, Miss Fairley. Good afternoon."

Emma barely had time to get to her feet before Lord Yeatman had taken his leave of them all. Even her mother appeared astonished, though Martha remained exactly where she was, sipping her tea and not looking at anyone save for Lord Wellbridge. Emma, seeing this, smiled softly to herself, and then sat back down, her happiness near to overflowing. Her sister was quite taken with Lord Wellbridge and now, it seemed, she might finally have a gentleman who was a little taken with her! But, she thought to herself, as her mother and Lord Wellbridge took their seats again, *he might very well have asked to walk with me simply because he has something more he wishes to say as regards my present situation.* Her smile faded. *There might not be any genuine interest there whatsoever.*

"Do you know, I have not seen Lord Yeatman in many a year!" Lord Wellbridge interrupted Emma's thoughts, making them all turn their attention to him. "He is a very wealthy Viscount, by all accounts."

"Wealthy?"

Lady Follet's eyes widened, and Emma groaned inwardly, already able to decipher what it was that she was thinking.

"Are not all titled gentlemen wealthy?" Martha interjected, her smile a little terse as she shot a look towards Emma which Emma did not at all understand. "Though some more than others, of course!"

"Of course," Lord Wellbridge chuckled, waving a hand. "Though for a Viscount, Lord Yeatman carries more wealth than some Earls! Though, Miss Fairley," he continued, looking towards Emma as his expression became serious. "Even though you have accepted the offer of walking with him tomorrow, I should encourage you to make certain of his character."

Emma's eyebrows lifted as Lady Follet snatched in a breath.

"You mean to say that there is something indecent about him?" Lady Follet asked, in a half-whisper. "Should I have stepped in? Ought I now to prevent this–"

"No, no, that is not what I mean in the least!" Lord Wellbridge exclaimed, laughing, and shaking his head. "It was only as a general warning to the young lady. I do not know Lord Yeatman very well at all, as I have said."

"I think him a very considerate and amiable gentleman." With a slight lift of her chin, Emma looked at Lord Wellbridge steadily, seeing him shrug. "But thank you for your... warning. My mother and father have said much the same to both my sister and me previously."

"Though we have nothing to worry about when it comes to you, of course," Martha said, with a laugh that made Lord Wellbridge beam at her with obvious delight. "Thank you, Lord Wellbridge. You are *most* considerate."

Emma picked up her teacup and said nothing more, taking a delicate sip and then setting it back down again. Her sister could have the most marvelous time making all sorts of remarks and conversation with Lord Wellbridge but Emma, for her part, would remain silent and consider all that had just taken place, wondering just what it was that Lord Yeatman wanted to speak with her about tomorrow.

CHAPTER TWELVE

I cannot quite believe I am waiting for a young lady to walk in the Park with me.

Frederick let himself smile as he shook his head lightly. The desire to see Miss Fairley again, to speak a little more at length with her, had come about shortly after their discussion in the ballroom, and her agreement that he might seek to assist her in some way. The more he had considered it, the more pleasant a situation it appeared to be. Even though he had nothing further to say on the matter of her supposed clumsiness, even though there was no sudden change of which he had to speak, Frederick had found his desire for her company growing steadily. Thus, he had decided – much to his surprise – to take the trouble to call upon her and ask her to walk with him for, that way, he had decided, he would be able to be in her company and able to make free conversation, without any concern that they would be overheard. *That* was what he wanted. He wanted to be able to talk to the lady simply so that he might know her better and, though he did not fully understand his reasons for it, it was enough of a desire to push him forward into action. Thus, he had called upon her, the arrangement had been made and now he was standing at the entrance to the Park, waiting for her arrival.

"Good afternoon."

Frederick turned around, his eyes narrowing as he caught the way a grin was edging up across Lord Gibson's lips.

"Lord Gibson. Good afternoon."

"Good afternoon," his friend said again, one eyebrow lifting. "Might I ask if you are doing anything... in particular?"

"What do you mean?"

"I mean that you are standing by the entrance to the Park and looking as though you are expecting someone."

Frederick chuckled, shaking one finger in Lord Gibson's direction.

"Ah yes, you have found me out. I am waiting for Miss Fairley."

Lord Gibson's smile immediately fell away.

"Miss Fairley? The one who—"

"Yes, the one who spilled that tray of drinks," Frederick confirmed, quickly. "But I do not think that it was her doing. However, I am simply walking with her through the Park, that is all."

"Because you would like to spend more time in her company?"

Frederick considered this and, with a shrug, nodded.

"Yes, I suppose so. I should like to spend more time in her company." Choosing not to say anything about her clumsiness and his own considerations in that regard, Frederick smiled as his friend's eyes widened. "Why should you be as surprised as that?"

"Because you are not often inclined towards pursuing a friendship so quickly," came the reply. "You are considered, you are cautious, and you are hesitant – and yet now I see you intending to go out walking with a young lady you cannot have known for more than a few weeks?"

Frederick considered this, tilting his head a little.

"I suppose that is true."

"Then what is your explanation?"

With a shrug, Frederick turned away from his friend, hearing a carriage approaching.

"I have no explanation other than that I should simply like to be in Miss Fairley's company for a time, that is all."

Lord Gibson put one hand on Frederick's shoulder.

"Well, do be cautious," he said, as Frederick watched first Lady Follet and then Miss Fairley descend from the carriage, soon followed by her sister. "You may find yourself flat on the ground or terribly winded depending on what accident she brings about!"

Frederick scowled and went to tell Lord Gibson that he had no expectation of such a thing, only for his friend to laugh and then turn away, leaving him to stand alone and wait for Miss Fairley to come closer. Evidently, Miss Fairley's mother and sister had come together to accompany her, though Frederick hoped that they would stay back from them so that he and Miss Fairley might speak in private.

"Good afternoon to you." Smiling, Frederick bowed

and then turning, offered Miss Fairley his arm. "It is a fine day for a walk, is it not?"

Miss Fairley nodded and managed a small, soft smile, but it did not light up her eyes. As Frederick considered her, as he took in the way her copper curls danced at either side of her face he wondered if she was looking a little paler than before.

"It is a *very* fine day," Lady Follet replied when neither of the Miss Fairleys spoke. "Now I, and my daughter, will walk behind you and Emma, Lord Yeatman. I hope that is acceptable."

Frederick nodded.

"But of course. I thank you." So saying, he turned and began to walk with Miss Fairley, feeling her hand tighten a little on his arm. "Are you quite all right, Miss Fairley?"

She looked up at him. He saw her lips tighten for a moment as though she was considering what to say, only for her to look away again.

"Might I ask why you asked to walk with me, Lord Yeatman?"

A slight frown flickered across his forehead.

"Why?"

Miss Fairley's eyes turned to him again.

"Yes. Why?"

"Because... because I wanted to." That sounded rather foolish, but the more Frederick considered his answer, the more he understood it to be the truth. "I wanted to walk with you, Miss Fairley, so I might get to know you a little better. It is very difficult to speak with you when we are at a ball or soiree or some such thing, for there is always something else going on, or someone else eager to interrupt the conversation!"

"I see."

Hearing the slight lift to her tone, Frederick smiled and caught her eye.

"I thought that you wanted to speak of my current situation," she told him, as he nodded. "There is something more that you wish to say about that, then?"

Frederick shrugged lightly.

"Well, if there is something that you would like to speak of then, of course, but my true desire is to speak with you and improve our acquaintance."

"Truly?"

Seeing her a little surprised, Frederick nodded and then reached across to pat her hand with his own.

"But of course. Why would that astonish you?"

"After you came to call, there was a remark made, and since then, my sister..." Trailing off, she shook her head. "It matters not. I should not listen to such things."

"Very well." Frederick wanted to press her and demand that she tell him what had been said, but instead, he only smiled and continued to walk. "I assure you, Miss Fairley, my only desire is to be in your company. Though, if anything untoward should happen, you can be assured that I will take every notice of it!"

"I thank you." Miss Fairley looked up at him and then let out a slow breath which was followed with a smile. "Then what is it that you would like to speak of? What is it that you want to know of me?"

Frederick's heart swelled at the happiness which was now in her tone, the joy which was running through her expression. Whatever it was that had been troubling her, it appeared to have gone from her very quickly indeed.

"I should like you to tell me anything you wish," he said, making her laugh softly. "Whatever it is you desire to say, I should be more than glad to listen."

"Very well." Miss Fairley tilted her head for a moment and then smiled up at him again, her eyes like stars. "Though so long as you promise to tell me a little more about yourself also."

He grinned at her.

"Gladly," he swore and as she looked up into his eyes, the sunshine seemed to grow just a little brighter and Frederick's heart filled with a happiness which he had never truly known before.

∼

"A very pleasant walk, yes."

Frederick kept his smile polite, having come across a small group of gentlemen and ladies on their walk. Both Lord Wellbridge and Lord and Lady Pleasance had been standing there and when his friend had beckoned him to join them, Frederick had felt himself obliged to do so. Miss Fairley had dropped her hand from his arm almost at once, however, though she had been willing to join the group. Her sister and mother had also stepped in so that the small group was now a good deal larger than before.

"It is a *very* fine day," one of the other young ladies said, though Frederick could not quite recall her name. "Though I am a little surprised to see you without a parasol, Miss Fairley!"

Frederick looked quickly at Miss Emma Fairley, but she did not react in the least. It was then that he realized that the young lady had been speaking to the elder Miss Fairley, for she responded with a laugh and gave some response – but Frederick could not take his eyes from Miss Emma Fairley instead. She had not even flinched, had not even lifted her gaze to see if she *was* being spoken to. Instead, as a wallflower, she was well used to being ignored and, much to his sorrow, obviously expected it. How much he despised seeing the way that the *ton* ignored her! It was not as though she had been involved in any sort of scandal and ought, therefore, to be given the cut direct! She had done nothing worthy of their disapproval. His chest filled with a tight, hot anger, and Frederick let out a slow breath in an attempt to keep his features settled in this otherwise calm expression.

"Perhaps we should take our leave, Miss Fairley?" he suggested, turning a little more towards her, keeping his voice low. "What say you?"

The look of relief she gave him was more of an answer than she could have expressed with words. With a nod, Frederick began to turn away, murmuring a word of excuse, only for someone to speak his name.

"Lord Yeatman?"

Frederick turned back.

"Yes, Lady Sophia?" he asked, seeing the young lady's eyes flick to Miss Fairley and then back towards him.

"You are leaving us?" she asked, her eyes still darting from him to Miss Fairley and then back again. "So soon?"

"Yes." Seeing no reason not to be honest, Frederick

smiled and lifted his chin. "I am enjoying my walk with Miss Fairley and though the conversation and company have been very enjoyable, I would much prefer to continue it. Do excuse us."

"It is time for us to depart also," Lady Pleasance added, throwing a quick smile at Frederick. "Do excuse us."

Lady Sophia cleared her throat as most of the others in the group began to take their leave also, forcing Frederick's attention back towards her.

"But are you not one of the wealthiest Viscounts in England?" she asked her question so astonishing Frederick that his eyes rounded and his whole body tensed. "Why, then, would you walk with a wallflower?"

The shock of that question sent a cold flurry rushing over Frederick's frame and he shuddered violently, his mind whirring with all manner of thoughts. He could not quite believe that the lady had the audacity to ask such a thing, and his only relief was that so many of the gentlemen and ladies had already taken their leave - not many were left to hear her question. Lady Sophia, in her arrogance, merely lifted an eyebrow and offered him a tight smile.

Frederick's heart exploded with anger, and he took a step closer.

"Lady Sophia, it is no one's business who I walk with, nor should I expect anyone to comment on what I choose to do and who I choose to spend time with. I–"

What sounded like a stifled scream caught his attention and Frederick whirled around, hurrying forward only to see Miss Fairley picking herself up from the ground. He rushed to her, aiding her as she stood up straight, only to see tears begin to drip onto her cheeks.

"I am so ashamed," she whispered, her eyes closing as she leaned into him. "Forgive me, Lord Yeatman. I have embarrassed you."

CHAPTER THIRTEEN

*E*mma did not know what had happened. One moment she had been walking slowly away from the group back towards the path and the next, surrounded by those who had been a part of the group, she had found herself on the ground.

Her knees stung, her palms ached and no doubt, her gown was ruined. The strong arms that helped her up and the whispered words of concern in her ear were something of a balm, but her injuries were more than just outward.

"I am so ashamed," she whispered, finding herself leaning into the strength that Lord Yeatman provided. "Forgive me, Lord Yeatman. I have embarrassed you."

"Embarrassed *me*?" Lord Yeatman's arm was around her shoulders now and though Emma was vastly appreciative of his comfort, she could not bring herself to look into his eyes. "You have done nothing of the sort. Are you quite all right?"

Emma dared a glance down at her gown and, much to

her surprise and relief, there did not appear to be any real damage. Yes, there were a few marks and stains from where she had fallen, but there were no rips or tears. That was a good thing, at least. Her gloves, however, had not fared as well.

"Oh dear." Wincing, she pulled them off carefully, seeing the tears which would have to be repaired. Either that or they would need to be replaced entirely. Her palms were very red indeed, but there were no cuts or scrapes to be seen.

"I shall replace them for you." Lord Yeatman took them from her without a word and then placed them in his pocket before returning his attention fully to her. "Can you walk?"

She nodded.

"Where are your mother and sister?"

Finally able to lift her head, Emma looked all around but could not see them. What she *did* see, however, was two of the ladies looking back at her, with one whispering behind her hand to her companion, who then turned to look directly at Emma without even a momentary hesitation. She closed her eyes and dropped her head, mortified that such a thing had happened yet again.

"I see them." Lord Yeatman took her hand and set it on his arm. "There they are, just ahead of us."

Emma swallowed sudden, threatening tears, and walked alongside Lord Yeatman, doing her best not to look at any of the other lingering gentlemen or ladies.

"Mayhap they did not see me stumble."

Lord Yeatman looked at her.

"Is that what happened? Did you stumble?"

Hesitating before she answered, Emma slowly shook her head.

"I cannot say for certain, Lord Yeatman. I do not know exactly what happened. Everyone was walking away, and I was taking only a few small steps to permit you the opportunity to continue your conversation with the lady you were speaking with when…" Closing her eyes for a moment, she shook her head. "I am so very sorry."

Lord Yeatman stopped suddenly, the surprise forcing her to look into his face.

"No," he said softly, though his face was set with a firmness which surprised her. "You have nothing to apologize for. You did nothing wrong."

"I brought shame upon myself by my ungainliness," Emma said, tears still threatening. "I did not mean–"

"I do not think you did anything." Lord Yeatman still spoke with a steady determination in his voice which Emma had no choice but to listen to. "Recall, we both believe that there may be someone who is attempting to do this *to* you for whatever reason, do we not? Why, then, should you think that your falling is simply your own doing?"

Emma's heart slammed hard into her ribs as she looked back into Lord Yeatman's face and saw his eyebrow lift just a little.

"I… I had not thought of that." In her mortification and shock, she had not thought for a moment that she could put the blame upon someone else. Instead, she had taken the full weight of it onto her shoulders. "But that would mean that someone here, someone who was present—"

"Deliberately did such a thing, yes." Lord Yeatman continued to walk, albeit a little more slowly this time. "That is rather significant, do you not think?"

"I suppose that it is." Emma sniffed lightly, aware of the ache in her knees, but finding that her heart was a little lighter. "Goodness, I had not thought that it would be someone present *here*."

"Though while that does simplify things a little, it does still leave us with a significant number of gentlemen and ladies. Did you know most of them?"

"All of them," Emma replied, slowly, going through every face present and recognizing that yes, she had been acquainted with them all. "Though we can safely discount Lord and Lady Pleasance."

At this, Lord Yeatman laughed aloud and that made Emma smile, despite her mounting worries.

"Yes, that is quite true," he agreed. "They would do nothing to injure you."

"Then who would?"

Lord Yeatman's smile faded.

"I do not know. Though I should suggest that if you can, you write a list of those who were present, for that should help you."

Emma nodded slowly.

"I can do that."

"Lady Sophia did not appear to be particularly enamored of your presence," Lord Yeatman said, though he waved one hand as though to dismiss what he had said.

"That is not to say that there was anything that you had done to cause her dislike, only that–"

"I understand what you mean," Emma said quickly, not wanting him to become upset on her behalf. "What did she say to you when I was walking away?"

Lord Yeatman's face flushed, and he scowled.

"She spoke of my wealth and asked why, given that, I would then consider walking with a wallflower. I found her condescension almost more than I could bear! In fact, had I not heard you cry out, I would have said a few very firm things to her without hesitation!"

Emma smiled and leaned a little closer to him.

"Then mayhap it is good that I required your help, Lord Yeatman."

There was something in his expression that made her heart leap, though she could not quite understand it. Was the softness about his eyes something that spoke of tenderness? Or was it merely sympathy?

"I am only sorry it happened," he said, after a few moments of silence. "Though I am glad that you are quite all right." There came a slight flicker in his eyes as he held her gaze. "Might you wish to walk with me again on another occasion, Miss Fairley?"

The hope in his voice and the light in his eyes made her heart squeeze as a sudden warmth rushed right through her.

"You would like to walk with me again, Lord Yeatman?" She knew the moment that she said those words that it had been a foolish thing to ask, given the way that his eyebrows lifted, but her surprise was so great, she could not help it. "Even after everything that happened today?"

"Yes, of course." Lord Yeatman's voice was warm and wrapped around her in gentle comfort. "*Despite* what happened today, Miss Fairley, I should very much like to spend more time in your company." He tilted his head a little closer to her. "I do not think you clumsy or ungainly or the like. I do not believe for a moment that you are responsible for such things. Therefore, Miss Fairley, I should very much like to become better acquainted because, while I do have an eagerness to be of aid to you, and I certainly want to make sure that you are not treated unfairly, there is a genuine interest within my heart." He smiled. "Does that please you?"

Emma could hardly find the words to speak, given how much joy had suddenly flooded her. She nodded, her throat constricting.

"Yes, Lord Yeatman. I... I confess that I am quite delighted by it."

"Good." With a smile, he reached across and patted her hand as it sat on his arm. "But I shall still be watching you at any soirees and balls and the like, Miss Fairley. You need not doubt that." He glanced at her. "Are you to attend one this evening?"

Emma nodded.

"Yes. Lord Shuttleworth's ball."

"Then I shall be present there this evening," he said, firmly. "And you can be sure that if anything untoward happens, I shall be fully aware of it."

"You look very lovely this evening, Emma."

Emma blinked in surprise as her mother came to stand beside her.

"Mama?"

They had only just entered the ballroom, and Emma had fully expected her mother and sister to distance themselves from her almost immediately. Instead, Lady Follet had lingered, now tilting her head to regard Emma a little more.

"Yes, very lovely," she said, as though she needed to confirm that to herself. "I do not know what it is you have done, but there is a fresh beauty to you this evening."

"I quite agree, Lady Follet."

Emma, caught by surprise by the low voice behind her, started in surprise only to see Lord Wellbridge coming to stand by her mother and sister. He was wearing a broad smile and Lady Follet immediately laughed, though Martha did not so much as blink, as her adoring gaze was fixed upon the gentleman.

"Good evening to you," he said, inclining his head to each of them in turn. "How fortunate I am to have found you so soon upon arriving at the ball! I must beg for your dance cards, of course."

Martha quickly pulled hers from her wrist and handed it to the gentleman though Lord Wellbridge then looked to Emma with clear expectation written on his face.

Emma blinked.

"You... you wish to dance with me?" she stammered, her face growing hot. "Are you quite certain?"

"But of course! Why should I not?"

"Oh, Lord Wellbridge!" Martha put one hand on the gentleman's arm, shaking her head lightly as she looked up at him. "Surely you cannot have forgotten what happened the last time you stood up with my sister? She has decided to stay back from dancing precisely because of that reason!"

The heat in Emma's face intensified, spreading down through her chest and she lowered her head, not able to look at either her sister or the gentleman.

"Ah, but what sort of gentleman would I be without forgiving and forgetting – and giving second chances?" Lord Wellbridge laughed, making Emma lift her head in surprise, seeing the very same astonishment etched across her sister and mother's faces. "Come, Miss Fairley, I think it would only be fair for me to give you another opportunity."

"Well..." Seeing her mother's eyes flare and uncertain whether it meant that her mother wished her to accept or reject Lord Wellbridge's offer, Emma took the dance card from her wrist. "Very well, Lord Wellbridge. I thank you."

Martha shot her a dark look, but Emma could say nothing to her. Both her mother and her sister had expected her to refuse, but Emma had chosen to accept – surely anything else would be rude. Evidently, that had been the wrong decision.

"Wonderful. Then the country dance, Miss Fairley." Lord Wellbridge smiled and then handed Emma back her dance card. Emma took it with a murmur of thanks, though her stomach twisted with nervousness as she did so. "And the cotillion for *you*, Miss Fairley."

He handed Martha her dance card. Emma went to return her card to her wrist, but another voice stopped her.

"Might I also sign your dance card?"

The voice in her ear made Emma yelp with surprise, only to see Lord Yeatman smiling at her.

"Lord Yeatman." The warmth in her voice was evident even to her, but Emma did not care. The relief of being in his company again filled her as she handed him her dance card. "Yes, of course."

"The waltz is still free, I see." Lord Yeatman glanced at her and then signed his name there. "And mayhap the cotillion also?"

Martha coughed quietly, catching Emma's attention as Lord Yeatman wrote his name for the second dance.

"*Two* dances, Lord Yeatman?" she asked, as Emma blushed quickly. "My, my. That is... interesting."

"Is it?" Lord Yeatman sounded rather nonchalant, not responding any further to Martha's remark. "Lord Wellbridge, good evening."

"Good evening, Lord Yeatman. We find ourselves in company again, I see."

"We certainly do."

Lord Yeatman smiled broadly, though Emma clasped her hands in front of her and squeezed them tightly together, aware of the tension rippling through her. Surely her mother would be glad that Lord Yeatman was offering her such attention? With *two* gentlemen seeking to dance with her, then surely her mother might consider her to be a little less a wallflower now, surely?

"Ah, Miss Fairley, Lady Follet!"

Emma turned, seeing two gentlemen and a lady approaching, all of whom steadfastly ignored Emma and did not so much as glance at her. The happiness which she had felt quickly began to fade and she took a step back.

"Should you like to take a turn about the room? Or might I accompany you to find your friends?"

Emma smiled briefly, taking Lord Yeatman's arm, and glancing again at her mother and sister, though neither of them were looking in Emma's direction. *How quickly I am forgotten.*

"Lord Wellbridge wishes to dance with you also, then?"

Emma looked up at Lord Yeatman, catching the way that his smile took a moment to spread across his face.

"Yes, he does," she said, slowly, "though that means very little. He is interested in my sister's company, as you might very well have been able to surmise, given the time you came to call, and I am sure that he only offered to dance with me as a kindness."

"I see." Lord Yeatman's smile quickly flattened. "He is interested in your sister, you say?"

"Yes, I think so," Emma replied. "He has often been in her company both in this Season and in the last."

"But they are not courting as yet?"

Emma's lips pursed.

"No, not as yet," she admitted, a slight frown pulling at her forehead. "Lord Wellbridge certainly appears to be interested in her company, for he is always coming to speak with her or dance with her, and he has come to call on her on multiple occasions, but as yet, he has not asked to court her. I am sure that must be something of a trial to my sister, though she has not spoken to me of it." Seeing the quick look that he shot her, Emma gave him a small shrug. "We are not particularly close as sisters."

"I can imagine it must be difficult for you, when your sister is favored by your parents," he said softly. "Though I am glad that another gentleman has sought you out for a dance... though I am delighted that he did not take the waltz!"

Emma laughed at this and then, seeing her friends, turned towards them. Even though she was sure that her mother and sister would have something to say about her dancing with Lord Wellbridge, Emma chose to set that to one side and, for the moment, enjoy everything that this ball had to offer her.

~

"THIS DANCE IS GOING VERY WELL, IS it not?"

Lord Yeatman grinned at her as Emma laughed softly, glad that the nervousness that had flooded her as she had stepped out to dance was quickly fading.

"Yes, I suppose it is."

"And you have not fallen or slipped," he told her, as the dance continued on, his words ebbing and then strengthening as they stepped away and then came back together again. "Thankfully, neither have I!"

"I do not think that you would have any difficulties in that regard," Emma told him, though Lord Yeatman chuckled and rolled his eyes.

"You would be surprised to hear of my foolishness, I

am sure," he answered, making her smile. "I have stood on many a toe beforehand, though thankfully, I am a little more careful these days."

"I am glad to hear it."

Hearing the music begin to slow, Emma concentrated on her last few steps, a little anxious that she might still do something that would cause her embarrassment in the last few moments. The music came to an end without incident, however, and Emma blew out a breath of relief as she curtsied towards Lord Yeatman. He bowed to her and then turned to speak to the gentleman to his right, who had said something to catch Lord Yeatman's attention.

Making to step closer to him, though the floor was now very busy with ladies and gentlemen stepping this way and that, Emma let herself smile, relieved that all had gone well – only for something to jab in her side. Letting out a loud cry of pain, she spun around in search of whatever it was, only for the same pain to stab at her other side. Another cry broke from her lips but with all of the gentlemen and ladies passing her, she had no notion as to either what was happening, or who it was that had done such a thing to her. Aching spread up her sides and Emma gasped for air, her eyes flicking left and right as she saw the other ladies and gentlemen glancing at her, though many quickly began to whisper together. Emma's face flamed, though the pain within her still blossomed, and she struggled to even lift one foot from the floor. Soon, she realized, she would be the only one left standing alone in the center of the ballroom.

"Miss Fairley!" Lord Yeatman grasped her hand at

once and put it on his arm, though his eyes were searching her face, worry etched there. "Whatever has happened?"

"I – I do not know."

"You have gone very pale indeed." Lord Yeatman leaned a little closer to her. "Can you walk?"

"I can, so long as I can lean on you."

"Of course." Lord Yeatman began to walk slowly, and Emma went with him, her hand clutching at his arm, a dull pain still running right through her. It eased as she walked and soon, Emma was able to breathe without too much difficulty.

"I am all right," she said, looking up at Lord Yeatman again, seeing him frown still. "I am sorry for what happened. I did not mean to shriek in that way."

"What happened?" The low tone of his voice and the way his eyes held shadows made her breath hitch. "Whatever happened, it was done by someone else, was it not?"

She nodded, her heart suddenly sinking low.

"It is the first time I have ever really, truly realized that there is someone determined to make me embarrass myself. I cannot understand why."

"Nor can I," Lord Yeatman answered, though his eyebrows lifted just a little. "Might I ask what happened?"

"Something sharp pressed into my side." Having reached the safety of the back of the ballroom, Emma caught Miss Simmons standing close by and beckoned to her. "And when I turned to see what it was, it caught me again on the other side."

Miss Simmons drew close.

"I heard you cry out," she said, reaching out to take Emma's hand. "Are you quite well?"

Quickly, Emma explained what had happened.

"There was pain down either side of me, though it has lessened in its intensity now."

"Good gracious." Miss Simmons' eyes flared. "Why would someone do such a thing?"

"To embarrass her." Lord Yeatman rubbed one hand over his face, his expression very dark indeed. "It is clear now that whoever this was, they were determined to do *something* to have you mortified in front of the *ton*."

"And they succeeded, yet again." Emma closed her eyes briefly, just to keep a hold of her emotions. "I cried out so loudly that even Miss Simmons heard me!"

Miss Simmons squeezed her hand.

"But it was not your fault."

Lord Yeatman let out a heavy breath.

"It is becoming a little more serious, Miss Fairley. Someone is seeking to injure you now rather than merely embarrass you. What was it that was pressed into your side in such a fashion?"

Emma paused, then shook her head.

"I do not know."

"You will have to check your gown for any sign of damage," Miss Simmons suggested, her eyes quickly darting to Lord Yeatman. "Though not here, of course. I–"

"I felt it pierce my skin," Emma said quickly, sending her friend an apologetic look for the interruption. "Something small and sharp."

The gasp that came from Lord Yeatman sent his eyes wide as he turned, grasped her hand, and squeezed it hard. She looked at him, uncomprehendingly, wondering at his astonished look.

"Could it be…?" Trailing off, he paused and then nodded as though he were confirming the idea to himself. "Could it be a hairpin?"

Emma's heart slammed hard against her ribs, and she too snatched in a breath, her eyes rounding.

"It could be, yes!" Miss Simmons exclaimed, answering on Emma's behalf. "That would make sense, would it not?"

"Yes." Emma pressed one hand to her stomach, her whole body going suddenly cold. "Which means that whoever is pursuing me in this way, whoever is eager to embarrass me, must be a lady."

Lord Yeatman nodded, his gaze melding to hers.

"An eligible young lady, for there were no married ladies dancing with us," he told her, steadily. "That list of yours, the one you made after our walk together in the park, do you still have it?"

Emma nodded, a slight trembling rushing over her.

"Then you may strike every gentleman from the list." Lord Yeatman's voice dropped low. "You are even closer to finding the truth, Miss Fairley. Soon, I am convinced, you will find out the name of this person and be done with this matter forever."

CHAPTER FOURTEEN

Frederick scowled darkly.
"I am not in the right frame for teasing, Lord Gibson."

Lord Gibson's eyes flared as he sat opposite Frederick at White's.

"Goodness, old boy. You are in something of a despondency."

"Who is in a despondency?"

Frederick looked up as Lord Pleasance set one hand on the back of Frederick's chair.

"Ah, good evening, Pleasance. Please, do sit down."

Lord Pleasance did so at once, sitting back in his chair, his legs stretched out and crossed at the ankle. His gaze flicked from Frederick to Lord Gibson and then back again, the slight smile on his face and the way he arched an eyebrow telling Frederick that he was a little intrigued.

"Lord Gibson was just asking me about Miss Fairley." Seeing that he was not about to get away without a proper explanation, Frederick shrugged his shoulders. "I am not particularly inclined towards conversation in that regard."

"No?" Lord Pleasance's eyebrow lifted higher. "But I thought you would be delighted to talk about a young lady who has caught your attention so intensely."

Frederick managed a smile, but it did not spread very far. After what had happened at the ball earlier that evening, he had not found himself in high spirits. His thoughts had turned continually to Miss Fairley, worrying about what might happen to her next, given that things had become a little more severe.

"What is it that troubles you?" Lord Gibson sat a little further forward in his chair, looking at Frederick expectantly. "You are not pretending that you do not like Miss Fairley but yet you do not wish to talk about it, and you do not smile either! It cannot be that the lady has refused you?"

"Refused me?" Frederick looked at his friend sharply. "What do you mean?"

"You *have* asked to court her, have you not?" Lord Gibson looked a little surprised when Frederick shook his head. "Oh. I thought that, given your interest in her, you might have done such a thing."

Frederick blinked and then threw back the rest of his whisky before ordering another, waving his hand at the footman. He had not thought about courtship but the more that he considered it, the more he realized that there was no particular reason why he ought not to do such a thing. After all, he was fully aware that he did care for the lady, that he was certainly not only concerned for her but drawn to her, so why should he not pursue something a little more intimate with her?

"Yes, I think I shall." Seeing his two friends shoot a look at one another, Frederick managed a wry smile and then shrugged his shoulders again. "It does not matter to me whether or not you know of my intentions. Yes, I will admit that previously I have never had any real interest in pursuing a young lady with thoughts of matrimony and the like, but that was all *before* I met Miss Fairley."

"Good gracious." Lord Pleasance blinked in evident surprise but then smiled. "That is quite wonderful. Miss Fairley does seem to be an excellent young lady, with a very delicate character."

"Though is she not still a little... ungainly at times?"

The question Lord Gibson asked sent a sudden fire rushing through Frederick's frame.

"No, she is not."

"No?"

Telling himself that Lord Gibson's question was not something that was asked out of spite, Frederick took a steadying breath and accepted the glass of whisky from the footman.

"The ungainliness is not her doing." Seeing his friends' slightly confused expressions, Frederick chose to give them both a brief explanation. "At your dinner, Pleasance, there was something that occurred that upset the calmness of the evening. Do you recall?"

Lord Pleasance nodded.

"The footman and the plate which slipped."

"I took responsibility for it, for if I had not, the blame would have fallen on Miss Fairley. Even though the footman would have been chided about being a little less than careful, the others at the table would have suspected that Miss Fairley had done something which had upset the plate."

"Because she is a little clumsy, yes," Lord Gibson said, though without malice. "The time the tray of drinks fell from the footman's hand was only because *she* reached for a glass and then–"

"And then what?" Frederick challenged, quickly. "What was it that you saw her do? What was it that she did that caused that entire tray to come crashing down?"

Lord Gibson hesitated, opened his mouth, and then closed it again.

"You see?" Frederick said, quickly, "You do not know. You cannot say what it was that she did, because she did not do anything. There is someone else, someone attempting to make it appear as though she is nothing short of awkward and graceless when, in truth, she is just as poised as any other young lady."

Lord Pleasance frowned heavily.

"I do not understand. She is a wallflower. Why would anyone demand that a wallflower appear so?"

"That is the reason she *became* a wallflower," Frederick explained, bringing understanding to them both. "The incidents which occurred last Season, and then again this year, seemed to be reason enough for her to be set aside, to be pushed away. Once she was set at the sides of the ballroom, once she was no longer in society's view, those incidents stopped. But," he finished, his stomach tightening as he recalled what had happened, "once she began to step forward into society again, those incidents have begun again."

"I see." Lord Gibson put out both hands. "I must apologize, then, for what I was led to believe. I ought not to have said that she was this or that way, if it was not her own doing."

"It seemed as though she was as you described, so I do not hold anything against you," Frederick said quickly, though silently relieved that his friend had accepted his explanation so quickly. "However, as I have known her a little better, I have seen just how badly someone is seeking to have her removed from society. Last evening, for example, someone pushed a hairpin into her sides, one at a time, so that she cried out so loudly, half the guests became aware of her!"

"Goodness." Lord Pleasance's eyes widened. "Is she quite all right?"

Frederick nodded.

"Later that evening, after consulting with Miss Simmons, she informed me that they had found a hole in either side of her gown, where she believes the hairpin would have been pushed into her sides. It did not do her any lasting damage, however, for which we are all grateful."

"Though that does sound rather serious," Lord Pleasance continued, quickly. "What is it that can be done to prevent this? Surely her parents–"

"Lord and Lady Follet have repeatedly pushed her back into being a wallflower and they do not believe that she is not responsible for what has happened," Frederick explained, quickly. "They will do nothing."

"Then you feel responsible." Lord Gibson's expression had become a little darker, perhaps a little guilty over what he had expressed about Miss Fairley previously. "You want to be of aid to her."

"Of course I do!" Frederick exclaimed, "Though my trouble is, at present, that I have very little thought about what I *can* do." Looking at each friend expectantly, he saw them both shake their heads and let out a small sigh of his own. "I wanted to be of aid to her. I wanted to help her and now, though we have discovered something significant, I cannot do anything further to assist her."

"Mayhap what you decided to do only a few minutes ago would be enough," Lord Pleasance said, quietly. "Have you thought of that?"

"I do not know what you mean." Confused, Frederick looked back at Lord Pleasance. "What was it I decided?"

"To consider courting Miss Fairley," came the reply. "That might be a support enough."

A smile tugged at Frederick's features as he thought of asking to court Miss Fairley. It would bring him a good deal of satisfaction and happiness, certainly, and he would have to hope that she felt the same way too.

"It is a good thought, certainly."

"She will feel a good deal of support from you in that regard, I would agree," Lord Gibson remarked. "You are showing her that you do not think of her as a wallflower – though you are doing that already. You are proving it, mayhap, and showing the *ton* that you think her worthy of attention."

"That is true," Frederick considered. "Though I would do it primarily for myself. I do care for the lady, and I cannot see what reason I have to step back from that. Thank you both for bringing that awareness to me."

Lord Gibson and Lord Pleasance both smiled and for the first time since he had stepped into White's, Frederick let a broad, contented smile settle onto his face. As soon as he had the opportunity tomorrow, he would go to call on Lord Follet and, thereafter, speak to Miss Fairley. He could only hope that she would accept him.

∽

"Lord Yeatman, how very pleasant to have you call."

Frederick smiled and inclined his head.

"I thank you."

"Please, sit down." Lord Follet sat down opposite, before gesturing to the table where the whisky sat. "Should you like something to drink?"

Glancing at the window where the sunshine streamed through, Frederick shook his head.

"A little too early for me, Lord Follet. Let me get straight to the point, if I may. I have come to speak to you in the hope that I might court your daughter."

Lord Follet's eyes widened.

"I see."

"It may come as something of a surprise, I am sure, but I will not be put off from this," Frederick said, firmly. "We have not been acquainted for long, but I have a consideration for her which I believe will grow into something all the more wonderful. That is the reason I wish to court her."

Lord Follet ran one hand over his chin though, much

to Frederick's surprise, he did not appear to be overly delighted with this suggestion.

"That is a good thing to hear, Lord Yeatman," he said, slowly. "I am always eager to make certain that any gentleman who shows an interest in my daughters does so with the right intentions."

"Which, I assure you, I have," Frederick said, quickly. "My intentions are not simply to court and then break things off once I have enjoyed a little more of her company! My sights are set solely on the future and in that regard, I will court Miss Fairley – should I be granted permission – with the view to betrothal and marriage."

"I see," Lord Follet said again, though a slight frown flickered about his forehead, confusing Frederick with the gentleman's lack of delight. "I shall have to speak to my daughter about this, you understand. It will have to be her decision."

Frederick frowned.

"I am well able to accept whatever answer she gives me. There is no need for you to concern yourself, Lord Follet. I will not demand that she accept me."

Lord Follet's smile was a little tight.

"It is not that, Lord Yeatman," he said, speaking with great consideration as though every word had to be chosen carefully. "You may not be aware of this, but my daughter has other gentlemen who are interested in her company. I would not want to presume on her behalf."

Frederick's chest tightened.

"I... I was not aware of that." Searching his mind for who these other gentlemen might be, Frederick found himself struggling to come up with even one single name. "Then I shall, of course, leave you to speak with Miss Fairley. I do hope that her answer will be a positive one, however." Getting to his feet, he shook Lord Follet's hand. "I admire Miss Fairley a great deal, Lord Follet. Ever since we sat together at Lord Pleasance's dinner, I have found myself quite captivated with her. Thank you again for your time in listening to my request." He released Lord Follet's hand. "Good evening." A slightly strangled sound came from Lord Follet's mouth, causing Frederick to pause. Lord Follet's eyes had rounded, and he did not appear to be able to speak, though he was shaking his head and blinking rapidly. "Are you quite all right?" Frederick turned back from the door. "Lord Follet?"

"You..." Lord Follet shook his head and then coughed. "Forgive me, Lord Yeatman. Am I to understand that you are eager to court my younger daughter, Miss *Emma* Fairley?"

Frederick nodded slowly, realizing now that Lord Follet had thought him to be interested in the elder daughter.

"Yes, Lord Follet. Forgive me if I had not made that clear. I have been spending a good deal of time with your younger daughter and I would, therefore, be eager to court her."

Lord Follet stared at him and then, much to Frederick's surprise, began to laugh. He laughed so hard that he began to wheeze, and Frederick worried he would have to soon ring the bell and call for some assistance. Eventually, however, the gentleman managed to contain himself and, to Frederick's astonishment, slapped one hand on Frederick's shoulder.

"My dear sir, if you had said from the beginning that it was Emma you wished to pursue, I should have taken you by the hands and danced a jig!" Lord Follet exclaimed, a clear delight in his expression. "Yes, of course, you may court her."

Frederick swallowed hard, finding his frustrations beginning to rise given how differently this gentleman treated his two daughters.

"I thank you," he managed to say, though he was not able to force a smile. "That is very much appreciated."

"Of course, you are aware that she can often cause you embarrassment?" Lord Follet asked, dropping his hand from Frederick's shoulder. "You will have seen it by now."

His back stiffened and it took all of Frederick's strength not to respond with a sharpness which would cut through Lord Follet's smile.

"I have not seen anything which concerns me," he said, firmly. "Thank you again, Lord Follet. If I may, I shall take my leave and go in search of your daughter."

"But of course!" Lord Follet seemed almost jubilant now, accompanying Frederick to the door and opening it for him as though he were ushering out a very special guest. "I ought to be the one thanking *you*, Lord Yeatman! You have truly made my heart happy."

Frederick murmured something incomprehensible and quickly took his leave, finding himself caught between relief and frustration. Lord Follet had not stated that he would have to ask his daughter about her opinion on the matter before accepting him, as he had done for his elder daughter. Instead, he had practically thrown Miss Fairley into Frederick's arms, and had she been present, Frederick was quite certain that was what would have happened.

It does not matter, he told himself firmly, making his way to the drawing room. *All that matters is that I have Lord Follet's agreement. Now all I need is Miss Fairley's acceptance.*

CHAPTER FIFTEEN

"I do not know *why* you agreed to dance with Lord Wellbridge!"

Emma rolled her eyes as she, Martha, and their mother all sat quietly in the drawing room, waiting for Lord Wellbridge to call. He had written a short note earlier that day stating his intention to come to visit and, of course, Martha had done nothing but express hope and delight ever since.

"It was not as though I could have refused, to do so would have been unforgivably rude."

"Yes, you could have refused him, and you ought to have done!" Martha railed, pinpricks of color in her cheeks. "It was foolishness to see a wallflower dancing with a gentleman."

"You ought to have refused him," Lady Follet agreed, quietly. "Though it all went well, at least. That is a good thing."

"By that, you mean that Emma did not fall to her knees or trip over someone else," Martha stated, a little coldly. "It cannot happen again, Emma. If Lord Wellbridge asks, then you *must* refuse him."

Emma lifted her chin.

"Why must I?"

Martha's eyes flared.

"Because–"

A slight rap at the door had them all straightening with Martha's face holding an expression of anticipation rather than frustration. Lady Follet called for the butler to enter and though he did come in at once, he was followed by none other than Lord Yeatman, rather than the expected Lord Wellbridge.

Emma quickly got to her feet, finding her face growing warm as he smiled directly at her. She could not help but smile back at him, her happiness growing with every moment. Suddenly, all that her sister had said about Lord Wellbridge – and all that she had been about to say – disappeared from Emma's thoughts completely.

"Lord Yeatman." Lady Follet curtsied as Emma and Martha did the same. "Good afternoon. Please, do join us."

"Thank you." Lord Yeatman took the proffered seat and then smiled again at Emma. "Good afternoon, Miss Fairley. Might I say that you are looking exceptionally lovely this afternoon?"

Her heart beat a little more quickly and though she could tell she was blushing, she did not look away.

"I thank you. I–"

"Lord Wellbridge, my Lady."

The butler, who had been told to permit Lord Wellbridge entry the very moment he arrived, interrupted

Emma's conversation and again, she rose to her feet and forced a smile as Lord Wellbridge came into the room. She curtsied, he bowed and greeted them all, though she caught the way his gaze lingered on Lord Yeatman.

"Again, it seems, we have come to call on the same young ladies, Lord Yeatman!" Lord Wellbridge exclaimed, coming to sit down as Lady Follet clicked her fingers to the butler, who quickly disappeared to have the tea tray brought in. "Forgive my intrusion. I do hope that I have not interrupted your conversation or the like?"

Lord Yeatman tilted his head, though his gaze slid to Emma.

"We were only just beginning a conversation," he said, with a smile. "It is nothing that cannot be continued."

"Indeed, indeed," Lord Wellbridge beamed, looking around at them all. "I have come to say just how wonderful the ball was last evening. I very much enjoyed dancing with you both."

"It was a *wonderful* dance," Martha sighed, as Emma kept her smile pinned to her features, wondering when she would be able to speak to Lord Yeatman again. "I do look forward to another dance, should you be so willing?"

Lord Wellbridge chuckled.

"I am certain I shall be, Miss Fairley," he agreed, as the tea trays were brought in. "There was nothing remarkable about either dance now, was there?" His gaze went to Emma who started in surprise, realizing that he was speaking about her dance with him and how nothing of concern had happened. "That was something of a relief."

Emma looked away, grateful when Martha got to her feet to serve the tea. Whether unwittingly or not, Lord Wellbridge had embarrassed her, and she did not want to acknowledge it in front of the others.

"Miss Fairley?"

She looked up, seeing Lord Yeatman's eyes searching hers.

"I am quite all right," she said softly, hoping that her sister's serving of the tea would keep them from hearing her. "I am well." Knowing that he understood and that he was concerned for her, she smiled as warmly as she could. "It is good to see you."

"I have just come from speaking with your father."

Emma's smile fixed itself in place.

"My father?"

Something chinked and Emma looked up sharply, only to see Martha's flushed face as she set down the teacup and saucer in front of Emma. Some tea had spilled into the saucer, which was something of a mishap – though Emma was not about to take her sister to task over it.

"Yes, I spoke to Lord Follet because I should very much like to court you, Miss Fairley."

This time when he spoke, Lord Yeatman's voice was a good deal louder as though he wanted everyone to hear him. Emma's whole body suddenly flushed hot, then cold, and then hot again, her eyes fixed to his. Courtship? Lord Yeatman wished to court *her*? She knew that there was an interest there, a consideration yes, but courtship was a good deal more serious than that. It was a consideration of their future, a look towards engagement and marriage... and was that what he was offering her?

"You... you wish to court Emma?"

Emma turned her head, looking into her mother's face, seeing the same wide-eyed, astonished expression as she was sure she was wearing.

"Yes, that is so." Lord Yeatman smiled and spread his hands wide. "I am sorry that I must ask in such a fashion when everyone is together, but I found I could not wait." Looking back at Emma, he sat a little further forward in his chair in clear expectation. "I should have waited to speak to you at the next social occasion we shared together, but my desire to ask you was a good deal too strong for me to hold back. Forgive me for that."

"There is nothing to forgive." Hearing the hoarseness of her voice, Emma clasped her hands tightly together, aware that she was shaking slightly. "Are you quite certain, Lord Yeatman?"

"That is a question that I should like to ask also." Emma did not turn her head but found herself frowning at her sister's sharp voice. Whatever was she doing in asking Lord Yeatman such a thing? "You are aware of her reputation, I presume?" Martha laughed harshly, the sound ripping the joy away from Emma's heart. "Why, you will have to be very cautious every time you step out with her! She may trip over her own feet, just as she did in the Park when you were out walking together."

Emma closed her eyes, her shoulders rounding and her head dropping forward. She did not know what it was that her sister was attempting to achieve by saying such a thing but, all the same, it burned through her regardless.

"Martha, please!"

Much to Emma's relief, her mother spoke up, silencing Martha.

"Do excuse us, Lord Wellbridge," Lady Follet continued, as Emma shot the gentleman a quick look. "This is a little unexpected, so you must forgive our lack of decorum!"

Lord Wellbridge was frowning hard. His eyes were set on Lord Yeatman's and were, in fact, a little narrow. Emma could not understand it, wondering perhaps if the gentleman was irritated that Lord Yeatman had interrupted the conversation that had been flowing between himself and Martha.

"Not at all. I can see that this is a surprising development... surprising for myself also."

"Miss Fairley?"

Lord Yeatman's voice was quiet now, catching her attention and pulling it back towards himself.

"Yes?" When she looked back into his eyes, it was as though the rest of the world had fallen away. It was only the two of them, only the soft, blue eyes searching hers as he smiled tenderly, perhaps already aware of the answer she would give.

"Would you accept my offer of courtship?" he asked, as Emma's fingers tightened in her lap all the more. "I know it is a little unexpected but–"

"Yes, of course, I shall accept!"

Lord Yeatman beamed at her, and it took all of Emma's inner strength not to get to her feet and hurry over to him as though, somehow, they might begin their courtship within this very room! The desire to be in his arms, though she had never been granted such a privilege before, was so strong, that it quite stole away her breath and Emma suddenly looked away, fearful that such a desire would be written into her expression.

"How wonderful!" Lady Follet clapped her hands, sounding genuinely delighted as Emma smiled across the room at her. "That is truly delightful! I am very pleased to hear you accept, Emma. After all, it is not as though you were to receive any further offers."

Emma's smile dropped to the floor.

"I would not have said that." Lord Wellbridge cleared his throat and smiled, though it did not stretch very far. "Very good, Lord Yeatman. I hope your courtship goes very well."

Much to Emma's surprise, Lord Wellbridge suddenly got to his feet, his actions a little hasty and sharp.

"This was the wrong time for me to call," he stated, sweeping into a bow, his tea and cake forgotten. "I shall take my leave and permit this happy moment to be captured by you all. Good afternoon."

"Good afternoon," Emma echoed, though Martha stepped forward, as though to catch Lord Wellbridge's arm to pull him back. Martha spoke Lord Wellbridge's name, but all he did was turn his head, throw her a smile, and then continue to make his way from the room. Emma's heart softened in sympathy for her sister as Martha resumed her seat, her shoulders a little rounded, though she kept her head high and her chin lifted.

"That was most considerate of him," Lord Yeatman murmured, as Emma smiled at him, appreciating his warm compliment of Lord Wellbridge, and knowing that it would mean something to Martha. "Now, Miss Fairley, might we now consider what we shall do first? An ice at Gunther's, mayhap?"

Emma clasped her hands tightly together again, her smile stretching right across her face as she nodded. That was a joy she had never before experienced, and certainly never with a gentleman!

"That would be wonderful."

"Tomorrow?" Lord Yeatman looked at Lady Follet. "Would tomorrow afternoon suit?"

"But of course!" Lady Follet exclaimed before Emma could answer. "Tomorrow afternoon would suit very well. I can take Emma in the carriage and will make sure to stay a distance away though she will still be properly chaperoned."

Lord Yeatman smiled.

"But of course. I am looking forward to enjoying that ice with you, Miss Fairley."

Wishing she could express just how happy she was about their expected outing, Emma offered him a smile and then let out a small, contented sigh.

"As am I, Lord Yeatman. It cannot come soon enough."

CHAPTER SIXTEEN

Frederick walked, arm in arm with Miss Fairley, finding himself filled with nothing but delight. The way that she had accepted his offer of courtship without hesitation had thrilled him entirely and now, as he looked down at her, taking in her copper curls, the gentleness of her hazel eyes, and the light smile on her soft lips, he found his heart swelling with a tender affection.

It was all quite wonderful.

"That ice was delicious." Miss Fairley let out a small sigh of happiness and then smiled at him as they walked together along the London street, taking in the carriages that went by and nodding to one or two others who walked past them. "I very much enjoyed our conversation also."

Frederick smiled at her.

"It was nice to talk about things other than your current difficulties," he agreed, as her cheeks warmed just a little, though her eyes still held fast to his. "I was delighted to hear of your love for poetry and riding. Mayhap one day, we might go for a ride together?"

"I should like that."

With a nod, Frederick looked back at the road ahead, finding his heart beating rather quickly at the thought of being out for a ride with Miss Fairley. He could already imagine her her eyes flashing with laughter and excitement, her cheeks flushed by the wind, her curls dancing in the breeze.

"Oh, look." Miss Fairley's voice softened. "There is Lord Wellbridge, talking with Lord and Lady Pleasance. He was very considerate yesterday, was he not?"

Frederick cleared his throat, finding his stomach tightening just a little at the sight of the gentleman. While Lord Wellbridge *had* been considerate at yesterday's meeting, he had begun to wonder at a couple of things that Lord Wellbridge had said. It had not been any sort of truly troubling thing, but only a word or two that had made Frederick's ears prick up. Thereafter, he had found himself considering them and wondering at them, though he had set that all aside for his time with Miss Fairley.

"Lord Yeatman?"

Frederick looked at her, realizing that she was waiting for him to respond.

"Forgive me, I was lost in my own thoughts," he said, smiling quickly to reassure her. "Yes, he was *very* considerate. Though I was sorry to see that your sister appeared to be a little disappointed in his departure."

Miss Fairley sighed heavily.

"Yes, that is quite true. Martha has been captivated

by Lord Wellbridge for some time, though he appears to be interested in her company also. That being said, as I may have said already, he has not yet offered to court her." Her expression darkened a little, her eyes pulling from his, her lips flattening. "That is something which she is struggling with, I fear."

"And you think that she ought to consider someone else?"

Looking up at him, Miss Fairley hesitated, then shook her head.

"I do not know. It is hard for me to say, for my sister and I are not dear friends and thus, we have never spoken of such things. That being said," she continued, "even though we have not spoken of it, I personally do not like that Lord Wellbridge does not make any further steps in continuing with an intimacy with my sister. If he wishes to court her, then he should take steps to do that. Otherwise, she will continue to pine for him and hope that such a thing will soon take place, and thus might miss the opportunity to find *another* amiable gentleman to court her."

Frederick's heart softened all the more as he listened to Miss Fairley. She was speaking with great sympathy and understanding for her sister, even though she was not close to her.

"That must be difficult for your sister."

"I think that it is." Miss Fairley sighed again. "She does not speak very kindly to me at times, but I am doing my best to believe that it comes from a place of both disappointment and hope: disappointment that Lord

Wellbridge has not yet come to court her but also hope that he soon will do so."

"I understand." Frederick was about to continue to say more, wanting to ask another question or two, only for Lord Wellbridge to turn, see them, and immediately hurry towards them. On seeing them, Lord and Lady Pleasance came to join them also – something which Frederick was profoundly grateful for. After yesterday's conversation and visit, he found himself a little uncertain about Lord Wellbridge and his motivations.

"Good afternoon!" Lord Wellbridge beamed and inclined his head, looking first at Miss Fairley and then glancing at Frederick. "How very fortunate to meet you both this afternoon. I presume that you are out walking together? Ah, yes, I can see your mother a little distance away, Miss Fairley." He gave no opportunity for either Frederick or Miss Fairley to speak, continuing without hesitation. "It is a fine day for a walk, is it not? I thought to come out for a brief stroll, hoping that I should find excellent company. And see now, I have done so!"

"Good afternoon, Miss Fairley, Lord Yeatman."

Both Lord and Lady Pleasance smiled as they greeted them, though Frederick caught the flicker in Lord Pleasance's eyes. It seemed his friend understood that since Frederick was here walking with Miss Fairley, his offer of courtship had been accepted.

"Might I ask you something, Miss Fairley?" Lord Wellbridge threw Frederick an apologetic look. "It would only be for a few moments, and it is of a rather... intimate nature as regards... well, as I have said, it is personal."

Frederick looked at Miss Fairley, seeing her gaze dart to his. No doubt she was thinking the same as him; that this conversation might well be about Martha, given what they had previously discussed and thus, it came as no surprise to Frederick when Miss Fairley nodded her assent.

"Do excuse me for a few minutes," she smiled, nodding to Lord and Lady Pleasance, and then smiling at Frederick. "I will only be a few steps away."

Turning his head, Frederick wondered whether he ought to say something to Lady Follet, given that she had been chaperoning her daughter from a distance, but the lady herself was in conversation with an acquaintance and did not so much as glance at her daughter.

"So, I see that your offer of courtship has been accepted?"

Frederick grinned as Lord and Lady Pleasance shared a look.

"Yes, it has, and I am delighted," he said honestly, seeing no reason to pretend otherwise. "It is a joy. I had to first ask Lord Follet, of course, and I was afraid that he would refuse me!"

"Why should you think that?"

"Because he gave all manner of excuses," Frederick explained, "though it quickly became clear that he thought I was speaking of the elder daughter. Once I explained it was Miss Emma Fairley that I wished to court, he could not have given his consent more quickly!"

"That is a good thing, however," Lady Pleasance added, her voice quiet, though her smile grew quickly as Frederick looked back at her. "It means that when you seek out his consent to betrothe yourself to Miss Fairley, you can be fully assured of the answer!"

Frederick made to say at once that he was not thinking of such a thing as yet, only to stop himself as Lady Pleasance laughed softly, perhaps seeing his reaction. If their courtship went as well as their acquaintance had done thus far, why should he not consider betrothal and marriage? Miss Fairley had quite captured him, every moment with her was a joy, and the thought of ending their acquaintance brought such pain to him, he could not even let himself think of it for more than a moment or two.

"I think that you have chosen a very fine young lady." Lady Pleasance glanced around, though her smile began to fade. "I did hear from Lord Pleasance of what you have gleaned about her situation, however. That does seem rather troubling."

Frederick nodded.

"It has been, though I confess, we have not given that much thought these last few days! It will have to be considered all the more, however, for–"

"Where did Miss Fairley go?" Lady Pleasance took a step closer to Frederick, one hand going to his arm. "I do not see her."

Turning around, Frederick searched for either the young lady in question or Lord Wellbridge, but to his astonishment – and horror – found that he could not locate her. She had said that she would only be a few steps away but instead, she had disappeared entirely.

"Lord Wellbridge's carriage is not here," Lord Pleasance growled, turning his head and looking back at Frederick. "It was there just a moment ago."

"But why would Miss Fairley sit in Lord Wellbridge's carriage?" Lady Pleasance asked, her voice a little hoarse with clear concern. "I do not understand."

"Because," Frederick gritted out, his concern about Lord Wellbridge's words previously coming back to him, "I imagine that he has a dark intention which he has not yet shared with anyone." Turning his head, he looked to Lady Follet, but she was still not looking at him, laughing at something her companion had said. "Yesterday afternoon, Lord Wellbridge said two things which made me wonder at his intentions. I considered them at length, in fact, but told myself they were of no concern."

"What was it that he said?" Lady Pleasance asked as Frederick ran one hand over his eyes, trying to work out what he ought now to do. "What concerned you?"

Letting out a hiss of breath, Frederick shook his head.

"He expressed surprise – his own surprise – that I had asked to court Miss Fairley, though to my ears, it sounded as though it held a little regret. Thereafter, when Lady Follet told her daughter that she would not have received any other offers of courtship, Lord Wellbridge shook his head and stated that *he* would not agree with that statement."

"As though he had intentions of courting the lady," Lord Pleasance said slowly, as Frederick nodded. "But why would he have refrained? Why would he have held himself back for so long?"

"I do not know. That is not important at present. What *is* important is that I find Miss Fairley."

"I would quite agree. But where will you look?" Lord Pleasance hurried forward. "Do you think he has taken her to his townhouse?"

Frederick closed his eyes as panic ran through him, his heart thundering furiously in his chest as he tried to keep himself calm and think clearly.

"I have no notion of where he has taken her – or why! I do not know what he means by this. I have never once imagined that he would do such an irresponsible thing as this – nor do I understand why."

"Take my carriage," Lord Pleasance urged him, gesturing to it and catching the driver's attention. "Hurry now. We will go and speak with Lady Follet and keep her distracted for as long as we can."

"I thank you." Without asking what it was they intended to do, or to say to Lady Follet to keep her in one place, Frederick rushed across the street to the carriage and climbed in, hailing the driver and telling him where he wished to go. Sitting back, he closed his eyes as sweat broke out across his forehead, panic still surging through him. The carriage moved forward – though not as quickly as Frederick wished – and soon was on its way to Lord Wellbridge's townhouse.

What is it that Lord Wellbridge wants with her? His heart clamoring with questions and concerns, Frederick ran one hand over his face, turning his eyes to the window. *And what will I find when I reach his townhouse?*

CHAPTER SEVENTEEN

"Might you step into the carriage for a moment?"

Emma frowned, looking from Lord Wellbridge to the carriage and back again.

"The carriage?"

"Yes, if you would?" Lord Wellbridge put one hand to his heart, letting out a prolonged sigh. "There is such a heavy weight upon my heart that I confess I *must* speak of it to someone."

Emma hesitated still.

"It would not be proper for me to sit in the carriage with only your company, Lord Wellbridge."

"Oh, but I shall leave the door wide open and as you can still see Lord Yeatman and Lord and Lady Pleasance from here, I am sure you can see that there is nothing to trouble you."

This was a little odd, Emma considered but, then again, there was something about Lord Wellbridge at this moment that caught her attention. He did have something he wished to share with her, she was sure, and given that it was no doubt about Martha, did she not have a sisterly duty to hear him out?

"I must speak to you," Lord Wellbridge said again, coming closer and lowering his voice. "Let me explain to you as clearly as I can." He took a breath. "After my hasty departure yesterday, I have taken a great deal of time to consider my... position in some things. I realize now that I ought to have stayed and taken advantage of that opportunity; I should have made my own intentions very plain. Instead, I departed and that was foolish. Might I have a few minutes to do so now? I will take full advantage of these quiet few minutes, I assure you. It will help my own heart a great deal if you would only be good enough to accept that from me."

Biting her lip, Emma took in another breath and then lifted her shoulders before letting them fall.

"Very well. So long as it is only for a few minutes, Lord Wellbridge. I am sure you can understand my concern."

"But of course." Lord Wellbridge swept into a great bow before her, catching her hand as he rose before inclining his head over it again. "You are very considerate and most generous, Miss Fairley."

"Whatever you wish to speak of must be of the greatest importance, I am sure," Emma replied, climbing into the carriage the moment he had released her hand. "Please, let us speak of it directly for I do wish to return to Lord Yeatman very soon."

Lord Wellbridge climbed up and sat opposite, only to reach across, pull the door closed and before Emma could protest, rapped on the roof. The carriage started at once and Emma snatched in a breath, a sudden fear enveloping her. Her hands dug into the seat as she stared at Lord Wellbridge, seeing him grin and finding herself suddenly terrified.

"Lord Wellbridge," she whispered, hoarsely, a weakness rushing through her now. "What is it that you are doing?"

"I am speaking with you, of course." Lord Wellbridge smiled as though it was more than acceptable for him to have captured her in this way. "Do you not understand yet, Miss Fairley? It is *you* that I wish to speak to."

Emma swallowed hard, her fingers still tight on the edge of the seat.

"For what purpose?"

"To make my intentions for you clear! Have you not understood them all this time?"

The eagerness of his expression, the wide eyes that searched hers, and the fierce hope that she would understand only added to Emma's confusion.

"Last Season, I attempted to seek you out, but your elder sister continually put herself in my way," Lord Wellbridge stated, rolling his eyes at the memory. "She has done so again this Season and then, for whatever reason, I have very rarely had the opportunity to see you or speak with you! I did not know why, and every time I spoke to your sister – for I sought her out very often in the hope of speaking with *you,* she gave no indication of where you had gone."

Emma's whole body went cold. She shivered involuntarily, looking back into Lord Wellbridge's face as she fought to understand what it was that he said. From what she understood, it seemed to be that this gentleman had been eager to pursue a courtship with *her,* rather than with Martha, as she had always presumed. That did not make the least bit of sense to her, for he had never made himself plain in that regard.

"You do not believe me." Lord Wellbridge sighed and then, reaching across, made to grasp her hand, though Emma snatched it back quickly and folded her hands across her chest, keeping herself as far from him as possible. Lord Wellbridge let out a long sigh and shook his head, seemingly a little upset that she did not trust him. "It is understandable. I must tell you that I found myself filled with such deep regret yesterday afternoon that I had no other choice but to take myself away from your company until I had thought through what I had to do next. Lord Yeatman has taken hold of you before I could do the same – but that is only because I could not find you! I danced with your sister very often, and asked her where you might be, and wondered why you had been pushed from society... in truth, however, I did think of my own reputation also." Wincing, he spread out his hands as the carriage trundled on. "You must understand, Miss Fairley, I am a gentleman with a title and reputation to take care of! I did not understand the reason for your absence from society. If some great scandal had occurred, then I feared that if I searched too hard, if I attempted to understand it with a little too much fervency, my reputation could be damaged. Therefore, I had to be cautious, though my intentions have always remained steady."

Emma closed her eyes, a thread of worry beginning to run through her veins.

"Lord Wellbridge, whatever your intentions were for me, surely you can see that what you have done at *this* moment is not at all proper! You are in danger of damaging my reputation."

"Ah, but now that you understand my feelings for you, there is nothing to concern yourself about in that regard!" Lord Wellbridge beamed at her as though this was the solution to her worries. "We can simply tell Lord Yeatman that you did not know of my feelings at the time that you accepted his courtship and–"

"I have no intention of accepting your courtship, Lord Wellbridge!" Emma stared straight back at him, seeing his eyebrows lifting. "I am perfectly contented with Lord Yeatman's courtship." Lord Wellbridge frowned, blinking rather quickly as though he had no understanding whatsoever of what she had said. "Though I do appreciate your consideration of me," Emma continued quickly, hoping that perhaps thanking him and showing some sort of kindness might encourage him to return her to Lord Yeatman. "However, I will not change my mind."

"But... but I am an Earl," Lord Wellbridge said slowly, his brows now so heavy over his eyes, they put shadows there. "He is only a Viscount. Why would you.... Ah, I understand." He shook his head. "Yes, I will admit that Lord Yeatman has a great deal of wealth, but my fortune is also quite substantial."

The carriage continued to make its way through London, and Emma looked out of the window, aware of just how quickly her heart was pounding as she struggled to find an answer to give him – an answer that would force him to turn around and bring her back from where he had left her.

"Lord Wellbridge," she said, firmly, lacing her fingers together and squeezing them tight. "It is not to do with Lord Yeatman's fortune, nor his title. Rather, it is because I think so very highly of him. He is kindness itself, has shown me nothing but generosity of spirit and–"

"All of which *I* can offer you also!" Lord Wellbridge exclaimed, reaching to put his hand on top of hers, though Emma pulled hers away. This, unfortunately, left his hand on her knee, and given the smile on his face, it did not seem that he was willing to give her even the smallest opportunity to escape him. "We do not know each other particularly well as yet, so you cannot compare me to Lord Yeatman. However, I promise you that I can be all that he is to you – and more!"

"No." Emma shook her head, tears beginning to burn in the corners of her eyes though she blinked quickly to push them back. "No, Lord Wellbridge. Though I can see that you are genuine in your attempts to convince me of your suitability, my mind is still made up. I chose Lord Yeatman, and I choose him again, despite your offer."

Lord Wellbridge's face went very red indeed. His eyes narrowed and he pulled his hand back, his jaw tightening hard.

"This will not do," he said, eventually as Emma's breath grew quick and fast. "This will not *do*, Miss Fairley! I cannot accept it. I *will not* accept it. We will continue to my townhouse and, thereafter, you will be convinced of my suitability."

"Please, Lord Wellbridge." The tears she had been fighting now began to run down Emma's cheeks though she quickly swiped them away. "My reputation is already damaged by being in your company alone. Please, do not risk it any further. It is not fair of you to do such a thing to me, it is not *right*."

"We will be able to court and eventually wed," Lord Wellbridge told her. "Your reputation, though it may be a little damaged by this incident, will not affect the outcome. I am sure that you understand and, though you may not be particularly pleased at this moment, I can promise you that you will find happiness again very soon." He folded his arms across his chest and turned his gaze to the window, refusing to look at her. "I will have you as my bride, Miss Fairley. It may happen a little more quickly than I had anticipated but if that is what must happen, then so be it."

"No," Emma whispered, looking at the carriage door and wondering if she could make her escape, though jumping from a moving carriage was not at all a wise idea, she knew. "Please, do not do this, Lord Wellbridge. Return me to Lord Yeatman and my mother. I do not want to court you. I do not want to wed you! The only person I care for is Lord Yeatman and I can promise you, he will not care one iota about this. Please, if there is any true tenderness of feeling within your heart for me, then–"

"No!"

Lord Wellbridge's face was scarlet as he swiped the

air between them with his hand, cutting her off completely.

"I have made my decision," he hissed, as the carriage began to slow though they were not anywhere near his townhouse as yet. "I will not have another word of protest from you, Miss Fairley. You will soon see that there is nothing to be gained by it. I always get what I want and, in this case, what I want is you."

Emma swallowed her tears, wiped her eyes, and shifted across the carriage so she was sitting as far from Lord Wellbridge as she could. Her heart was pounding furiously, her whole body shaking but her mind was clear. This was a truly desperate situation, but one where she *had* to find her way out. If she did nothing, then Lord Wellbridge would gain what he sought, and she would be left without a single modicum of happiness. What she had shared with Lord Yeatman would be broken apart, never to be recovered, and Emma cared about the gentleman too much to let that happen.

I must escape, she told herself, glancing across at Lord Wellbridge and seeing him remaining just as he had been, looking steadfastly out of the other window. Jumping from the moving carriage would not be a wise idea unless she wished to twist or break her ankle, but how else could she escape him?

At that moment, the carriage began to slow, and Emma heard what seemed to be a few distant shouts. She barely glanced at Lord Wellbridge, her eyes going to the door as she forced courage into her limbs. The trembling did not cease completely but it gave her enough conviction that she could do what was required.

It is my only chance, she told herself, as the carriage slowed all the more though did not stop entirely. *I must go now!*

Taking in a steadying breath, Emma blew it out slowly and then, in one swift movement, reached for the door. It opened and she flung it back, only to hear Lord Wellbridge shout her name. Pushing herself up, she tried to get to it, tried to leap from it to the cobbled street beneath, but Lord Wellbridge caught her arm and shouted her name again.

"Release me!"

A scream lodged in her throat as she grasped at the doorframe of the carriage, pulling herself as hard as she could away from Lord Wellbridge. Lord Wellbridge rapped hard on the roof and then, with his other hand, pulled her bodily back to the seat.

She had failed.

The door to the carriage was pulled open and another figure climbed inside.

"Release her, Wellbridge!"

Emma let out a cry of relief as Lord Yeatman's frame filled the carriage, coming between her and Lord Wellbridge. She did not want to ask what he had done, or how he had found her; all she could feel was relief.

"Now!"

Emma could not quite see what had happened, her vision was a little blurred at the edges given the shock and fright that ran through her. Hearing Lord Wellbridge's howl of pain, she blinked furiously, feeling his hand release from her arm.

"Come, Emma."

Lord Yeatman's hand was gentle as it took hers though she grasped it firmly, letting him take her to the door. He stepped out first and then helped her down, the carriage having come to a standstill.

The moment she stood on the ground, his arms were around her.

"Thank God, I found you." His voice was hoarse as he held her close and Emma sagged against him, tears threatening all over again. "I did not think... I was afraid that—"

"I am all right."

He released her, though looked down into her eyes, searching her face.

"I must return you to your mother before she realizes something is wrong," he said, quietly. "Lord Pleasance's carriage is just here. Come."

Emma struggled to put one foot in front of the other as she leaned heavily on Lord Yeatman's arm. It took the last few ounces of strength to step up into the carriage and the moment that she sat down, her whole body sank into the seat and she did not think that she would be able to rise again without help.

"We will be back with your mother very soon. I am hopeful that Lord and Lady Pleasance will have distracted her so well that she will not be aware of your absence." Lord Yeatman shifted from the other side of the carriage to sit next to her, and Emma rested her head on his shoulder, her chest heaving with the whirlwind of emotions that overcame her. "Did he hurt you?"

"No," she whispered, her eyes closing as she settled

against him. "But what he said is so astonishing, I do not think that I can speak of it."

"Then do not," he said softly. "I will have you returned home as quickly as possible but, until then, do not push yourself to say even a single word."

"Will you call on me tomorrow?"

He nodded, his lips brushing her forehead.

"Of course," he whispered, softly. "And every day after that, if you wish it."

She nodded, her throat tight.

"I wish it," she replied, only just managing to hold the tears back. "Thank you for saving me from him, Lord Yeatman. I do not know what would have become of me had you not."

"I would have been loyal to you no matter what had taken place," he swore, making her lips lift just a little. "Rest now. It will not be long before you are returned to your mother."

CHAPTER EIGHTEEN

"I will call on you tomorrow." Frederick offered Miss Fairley a small smile, relieved when she managed to return it despite the whiteness of her face. "I do hope that you feel better quickly."

"It was very good of you to take her back to Gunters and sit there with her, Lord Yeatman." Lady Follet glanced at her daughter as they sat in the carriage, with Frederick and Lord and Lady Pleasance standing together beside it. "I am only sorry that I was too distracted to notice!"

Thinking that this did speak of genuine concern for her daughter, which meant that Miss Fairley would be well looked after, Frederick gave Lady Follet another small nod.

"But of course. I would like to call tomorrow if I can."

"I look forward to it," Miss Fairley replied, despite her mother's concerned look. "Thank you again, Lord Yeatman. For everything."

He smiled and then stepped back, the carriage door

closing and, thereafter, driving away. Closing his eyes, Frederick blew out a long, slow breath and tried to calm the twisting anger that was whirling around his very soul.

"I am so very glad that you found her." Lady Pleasance put one hand on his arm. "What happened?"

"I do not know," Frederick replied, opening his eyes again to see the look of concern on Lady Pleasance's face. "But whatever it was, it was greatly upsetting for Miss Fairley. Thank goodness that the carriage came to a stop when it did! I practically leaped from my carriage and ran towards it and when I pulled the door open, I saw Lord Wellbridge with his hand around Miss Fairley's arm, pulling her back from the door. No doubt she was attempting to climb out and he was determined to stop it."

Lady Pleasance shook her head.

"How dreadful."

"I presume that we are going to go and speak with Lord Wellbridge?" Lord Pleasance lifted an eyebrow as the anger in Frederick's heart continued to burn. "He cannot be permitted to continue in this way."

Frederick nodded, his jaw tight.

"Certainly, that is true. If you are willing, then I am more than contented to go with you to his townhouse to see if we can... *speak* to Lord Wellbridge about what he attempted to do this afternoon."

"Husband." Lady Pleasance turned to Lord Pleasance, no doubt ready to tell him that he was not to do anything too harsh. "When you find Lord Wellbridge, please make certain to make my thoughts on his actions *very* clear indeed."

Frederick's eyebrows lifted, a slightly grim smile spreading across his face at her fervor.

"We shall make certain to do so," Lord Pleasance promised. "Shall we go at this very moment, Yeatman?"

Frederick nodded.

"If you please. Thank you, Lady Pleasance, for all that you did in entertaining Lady Follet. I do not think I would have been able to salvage Miss Fairley's reputation without your efforts."

"I was glad to do it," Lady Pleasance replied, quietly. "I do hope that she will be all right."

"As do I."

∼

"We would speak with Lord Wellbridge." Frederick lifted his chin as the butler glanced from Frederick to Lord Pleasance. "Now."

"I am afraid that Lord Wellbridge is not able to take callers at the present moment." The butler bowed. "I am sorry. Can I-?"

"We are going to speak with him whether he wishes it or not," Frederic interrupted. "Now, either you tell us where the gentleman is, or we will go and find him ourselves."

The butler's mouth opened and then closed again, his eyes still looking from Frederick to Lord Pleasance and back again, as though, somehow, he would be able to ascertain whether or not they were being honest. Frederick snorted and stepped forward, only for the butler to speak.

"If you were to search the house, you might find him in the study," he murmured, before melting back into the shadows.

Frederick lifted an eyebrow in Lord Pleasance's direction. When a gentleman's servants were so willing to set aside their loyalty to their master, it did not speak too highly of the gentleman himself!

"The study, then. Come, I know where it is. I was at a soiree here last Season." Leading the way, Lord Pleasance made his way down the hallway as Frederick followed him, attempting to control the anger that had not left him since he had first flung open the door of Lord Wellbridge's carriage. He could still see the fright on Miss Fairley's face, and that only added to his fury. "Here we are."

Without hesitating, Lord Pleasance opened the door and stepped inside and Frederick, following suit, saw Lord Wellbridge half rise from his chair, only to sit back down again, his face going rather pale.

"Wellbridge." Frederick stormed across the room and, leaning across the table, grabbed Lord Wellbridge by the collar and hauled him to his feet. "Would you care to explain what it is that you were doing with Miss Fairley, Lord Wellbridge?"

"Steady, old chap." Lord Pleasance put a hand on Frederick's arm and he released Lord Wellbridge, albeit a little unwillingly. Lord Pleasance fixed Wellbridge with a stern glare and spoke, his voice full of barely repressed anger. "So, Wellbridge. I hear that you are in the business of capturing young ladies in your carriage?"

Lord Wellbridge put one hand to his throat, gasping

and coughing, though both Frederick and Lord Pleasance remained unmoved. Eventually – perhaps seeing that he was not about to be given any sort of sympathy – Lord Wellbridge sat up straight in his chair and smoothed his shirt, though his face still remained rather pale.

"I was merely desirous to express my feelings to Miss Fairley."

Frederick's eyebrows shot towards his hairline.

"Your feelings?"

Lord Wellbridge lifted his chin.

"Yes."

Shock was like a knife through his chest.

"What are you talking about?"

"I have been interested in furthering my acquaintance with Miss Fairley for a long time," Lord Wellbridge said, his chin lifting as he shot a narrowed look back toward him. "I was uncertain about my interest last Season, though I did find myself continually drawn back towards her. This Season, however, I was determined to pursue her, only for her then to suddenly disappear from society events! I did not understand it and sought out her sister to find out where she had gone – without making myself too obvious, of course. I did not want to damage my reputation if there was something of concern."

"You... you were seeking to court Miss *Emma* Fairley since last Season?" Frederick could hardly believe his ears, for even though Lord Wellbridge had stolen Miss Fairley away, had pulled her away from her mother and even from him, he had never once suspected that Lord Wellbridge had held such a prolonged interest! The way that Lord Wellbridge had spoken when Frederick had asked Miss Fairley to court suddenly became clear. "Your interest appeared to be very firmly fixed upon Miss Martha Fairley."

Lord Wellbridge snorted and rolled his eyes.

"No, no, you are mistaken. Miss Martha Fairley was always more interested in my company than her sister but that did not mean that I reciprocated that! In truth, I found her – Martha, that is - a little irritating. She was always ready with a smile, hanging on my arm, expecting me to dance with her. I did, of course, but it was not without reluctance. Besides which, as I have said, I was doing my utmost to make certain of my feelings first, though I appeared to have taken a little too long." Scowling, his lip curled. "I wanted Miss Fairley to know that I was the better-suited gentleman for her. She did not know of my feelings and thus, I thought it only right to tell her."

"By stealing her away?" Frederick exclaimed, throwing up his hands, his anger returning swiftly. "By pulling her into the carriage and then holding her fast so that she could not escape?"

"She was always meant to have been mine!" Lord Wellbridge protested, his eyes wide as though Frederick simply did not understand. "Had I taken hold of my affections and considered them with a good deal more gravity and seriousness than I did, then she would have known of my intentions, would have accepted me, no doubt, and would never once have considered you!"

"That does not make what you did the right thing," Lord Pleasance growled, making Lord Wellbridge jerk in surprise, as though he had forgotten that Lord Pleasance was present. "How could you think to do such a dreadful act? You would have ruined Miss Fairley's reputation, had she been discovered!"

"But that would not have mattered," Lord Wellbridge protested, as though Frederick and Lord Pleasance did not understand. "Even if her reputation had been a little tarnished, I was already there, waiting for her to accept me. Nothing would have gone wrong! We would have stepped out into a happiness which would have lasted until the end of our days." The light smile on his face dropped away as he threw a scalding look towards Frederick. "But *you* had to ruin the situation for me."

"And I am glad that I did," Frederick stated, coldly. "Listen to me, Wellbridge." Leaning closer to the gentleman, Frederick stuck one finger into the man's chest. "You are *not* to go near to Miss Fairley again. In fact, you are not to draw near to either Miss Emma Fairley *or* Miss Martha Fairley. Your acquaintance with them must come to an end."

Lord Wellbridge shook his head no.

"I will not. I care about Miss Fairley. I will not let you—"

"Yes, you will." Straightening, Frederick stood tall as Lord Pleasance moved to stand beside him, presenting a united front against Lord Wellbridge. "And if you do not, then there will be great and heavy consequences."

"Such as?" Lord Wellbridge laughed aloud as though he was quite certain that, anything which Frederick and Lord Pleasance threatened, he would be more than easily able to brush off. "There is nothing that you can do. I—"

"I will call you out if you do not heed me."

Frederick's voice thundered around the room, making Lord Wellbridge's eyes flare wide.

"And I will be his second," Lord Pleasance said hastily, as Frederick kept his gaze steadily fixed on Lord Wellbridge. "No doubt many in the *ton* will wonder why such a duel is taking place."

The shock ran from Lord Wellbridge's face as he smiled darkly.

"Ah, but then you shall have to tell them all about Miss Fairley and think about what damage that will do to her!"

Frederick did not hesitate.

"I will," he said, slowly, "and what will the *ton* think when they discover that you attempted to steal away my betrothed?" He kept his gaze fixed on Lord Wellbridge, though he caught, out of the corner of his eye, the way that Lord Pleasance looked at him. Yes, he had not had any real intention of pursuing betrothal to Miss Fairley so soon, but if this was the way to protect her from Lord Wellbridge, then he was more than willing to do that. In fact, the more he considered it, the happier his heart became, despite the present situation.

"Your... your betrothed?" Lord Wellbridge began to stammer, pushing himself up straight in his seat. "Your betrothed?"

"Yes." Frederick lifted his chin. "My intention is now to propose to Miss Fairley and I have every expectation that she will agree and accept my offer. You see, Lord Wellbridge, what you have attempted to do has, in fact, only pushed Miss Fairley and I closer. It will not be that we are torn apart, not that we are set back from each other but instead, we are seeking to draw closer than ever before. My intention now is to propose to her so that she is secure, that she is safe, and that she is loved."

Lord Wellbridge swallowed hard. He did not look in the least bit pleased any longer and did not appear to be delighted with his intentions and plans. His eyes were fixed on Frederick, his face going a shade of red before he finally closed his eyes and then shook his head.

"No. She is meant to be courting *me*, not you."

"We are to be betrothed," Frederick stated, firmly. "You will not be able to come near her any longer, Lord Wellbridge. And because I care about her, I must also care about her sister – which means that you are now to consider your acquaintance with that family at an end. Otherwise, I *will* call you out and the *ton* will know of what it is that you have done."

Turning on his heel, Frederick made his way to the door, finding himself satisfied with all that he had said and all that he had done. Lord Wellbridge had not said a single word and, even as Frederick opened the door and stepped out, he still said nothing. Lord Pleasance followed Frederick, the door slamming closed behind them and Frederick let out a long, slow breath, pausing for a moment as he closed his eyes.

"That was done well." Lord Pleasance set a hand on Frederick's shoulder for a moment. "I think that Lord Wellbridge has been convinced."

"Do you think so?"

Lord Pleasance nodded as they made their way to the door.

"Certainly. He may not have been at first, but after

you spoke about your expected betrothal, I think that he understood the significance of your determination as regards calling him out should he go near Miss Fairley."

"Good."

As they stepped outside, Lord Pleasance turned again to Frederick, his eyes sharp.

"Did you mean what you said?"

Frederick frowned.

"What do you mean?"

"About proposing to Miss Fairley. After all," he continued, still looking a little concerned, "you have only just begun courting, and now... now you are thinking about proposing?"

Considering this, Frederick took a few moments before he nodded, and then, as his heart filled all over again with a great and profound happiness, he smiled.

"Yes, I am entirely serious. It is as I have said to Lord Wellbridge; I want to propose so that she is protected, she is safe but also so that she is loved." That sentence caused him to take a great deep breath, his chest expanding. "I am tired of seeing her being treated as though she is lesser, even though she has done nothing wrong. I am sorrowful at seeing her own family set her apart from her sister – again, because she has done nothing wrong. All these clumsy accidents, all these supposed awkward moments, have not come from her – and I will take her away from all of that and love her, care for her, and consider her in the ways she always ought to have been."

Lord Pleasance continued to search his face for a moment and then, with a loud exclamation of delight, slapped Frederick's back and grinned broadly at him.

"How wonderful! I am truly delighted for you. It may be a little sudden, yes, but I think that this is right. I see how happy you are in her company, and the fervency with which you pursued her when Lord Wellbridge had her speaks, I think, of the fervency of your feelings in your heart. You say that you wish to love her as she always ought to have been loved. Can I ask if that means that your own affections are strong?"

"I have not paused to consider them in depth but yes, I am certain that what I feel is very strong indeed," Frederick stated, firmly. "My intention is now to return home, to rest for the evening, and to let myself consider all of this. I will think about what I want to say to Miss Fairley, what it is that I truly feel for her, and what words are best to use to express that desire. I am convinced, however, that my feelings and affections are truly very strong indeed. They are growing, they are fervent, and they will, I hope, bring us both a new sense of happiness and joy."

"I am sure that shall be true," Lord Pleasance smiled, though a slight, flickering frown took that smile from him almost at once. "Though all of this does not answer one particular question, does it?"

A little confused, Frederick looked back at him.

"What do you mean?"

"About Miss Fairley and all the clumsiness," Lord Pleasance replied, with a scowl. "It does not answer anything in that regard, does it?"

Frederick bit his lip and then shook his head.

"No, it does not," he agreed, quietly. "That is something which still requires an answer... though I think I may know exactly who it was, and why it is that they have done this to Miss Fairley."

Lord Pleasance lifted an eyebrow in question, but Frederick shook his head.

"No, my friend. I will keep my own counsel until I have the opportunity to speak of it all with Miss Fairley," he said, as his friend nodded in understanding. "But you may wish me luck for tomorrow afternoon, yes?"

Lord Pleasance chuckled as they climbed into the carriage again, their task now completed.

"I do not think that you will require even the smallest measure of luck, my dear friend," he said, making Frederick smile. "I have every certainty that, by this time tomorrow, you will have Miss Fairley as your betrothed."

CHAPTER NINETEEN

*E*mma sat down in the most comfortable chair in the drawing room, letting out a long, slow breath as she did so. After yesterday's ordeal, she felt herself a little shaken still, but a good deal recovered... though if it had not been for Lord Yeatman's swift actions, she might well have found herself in a very different situation. The maid came in with a tea tray and set it in front of her and Emma murmured a small word of thanks before dismissing her. She was relieved to have a little quiet this afternoon. No doubt, Martha and her mother would soon come to join her, once Martha had finished her preparations for afternoon calls.

And Lord Yeatman will call upon me soon, Emma thought to herself, smiling. *What a joy that will be.*

The door opened quickly, stealing her solitude from her and Emma offered her sister a small smile despite the flickering irritation within her.

"Martha. You look quite lovely." Martha offered her a thin-lipped smile but said nothing, sitting down opposite

Emma and then eyeing the tea tray. "I am certain that many a gentleman will come to call upon you," Emma murmured, a little confused as to why her sister had remained silent and now appeared to be so sour-faced. "Though I should like to speak to you about Lord Wellbridge. I think–"

"Why should you have an interest in Lord Wellbridge?" her sister snapped, her eyes flashing with a fire that took Emma completely by surprise. "You are already betrothed, are you not? Why should you even *think* of him?"

"I.... I am not." Confused, Emma attempted to catch her sister's gaze, but Martha would not look at her, stubbornly staring somewhere around Emma's left shoulder instead. "I was only about to say that there is something about him which I should like to tell you about. I find myself rather concerned that you might still be considering him."

Martha let out a harsh, cold laugh.

"Is that so? And here I was, quite certain that you hoped he would be calling upon *you* instead. Was that not what you wanted? Is that not always what you have desired?"

Emma blinked, her eyes widening as Martha's furious gaze finally fixed on hers. She had very little understanding of what it was that her sister was saying, and was just about to ask her to explain when the door opened, and the butler stepped inside.

"Lord Yeatman has come to call, Miss Fairley."

Emma's heart leaped almost at once as she rose to her feet, the butler having been instructed to bring the gentleman in at once. When he walked into the room, Emma could not help but hurry towards him and, despite her sister's presence, stepped directly into his embrace and sighed with contentment as he enfolded her into his arms.

"My dear Emma," he said, softly. "How glad I am to see you." Stepping back, he caught her hands in his, but his eyes searched her face. "Are you quite well?"

"I am." Emma turned her head and let her gaze slide towards her sister, though Martha only scowled and looked away. "I have not yet spoken of all that has taken place, but I was intending to do so."

Something flashed across Lord Yeatman's face, something which Emma could not quite make out. He opened his mouth, seemed to think better of it, and then closed it again, giving her a small shake of his head before moving forward.

"Miss Fairley."

Smiling, Lord Yeatman inclined his head as he greeted Emma's sister, though Martha did not so much as get to her feet, making Emma frown hard at the ill manners displayed. She did not understand what had put Martha into such a dark mood, and certainly had no knowledge of what it was that Martha was attempting to express.

"Let me ring for a fresh tea tray." Going to ring the bell, Emma smiled as Lord Yeatman sat down on the couch, giving her room to sit beside him. "You cannot know how glad my heart is at seeing you again."

"I am filled with nothing short of relief and joy to see you so well," came the reply as he grasped her hand, clearly entirely unconcerned about Martha's presence and what she might think. "The ordeal you endured was a great one."

Emma swallowed the knot which had formed in her throat and gave him a small yet wobbly smile.

"I am quite well, I assure you. And there has been no difficulty as regards my standing or anything like that. Even my own mother is unaware of it."

This last part was spoken in hushed tones and though Martha frowned in Emma's direction, Emma chose to give no explanation.

"I have just come from speaking with Lord Wellbridge," Lord Yeatman replied, his voice not as quiet as Emma had hoped. "I spoke firmly with him and made it quite clear—"

"You... you have spoken to Lord Wellbridge about Emma?"

Emma glanced at her sister and then back to Lord Yeatman. She lifted her shoulders in a half shrug and then looked again at Martha.

"Martha, I did hope to speak to you about something specific though it would have occurred at a later time, rather than this afternoon. I know that you are expecting other gentlemen callers but mayhap to speak of this now would be wise."

Martha's eyes darted from Emma to Lord Yeatman and then back again.

"I do not know what you mean. There can only be one reason as to why you would have gone to speak to Lord Wellbridge about Emma."

Emma frowned.

"What do you mean?"

"You need not hide it from me!" Martha got up suddenly, throwing up her hands as she began to stride up and down the room, in short, quick steps. "I understand it all. I know of it all!"

"Know what?" Emma's frown grew deeper as she looked again at Lord Yeatman, though the way his eyes flickered told her that he understood more than she did at this present moment. "The reason Lord Yeatman went to speak with Lord Wellbridge is because of something rather serious which took place, Martha. Though, before I begin to explain, I should like your promise that you will not speak of it to Mother or Father. It is best for everyone that they remain unaware."

"But not best for me?" Much to Emma's astonishment, tears began to fall from Martha's eyes, splashing onto her cheeks, which were now deep red. "Do you not understand that I am already fully aware of this and it has caused me a great deal of pain?" Martha cried, dashing one hand over her eyes to chase away further tears. "I have watched Lord Wellbridge, I have seen everything, and I have found myself broken because of it." Emma blinked furiously, only for clear understanding to wash over her. Her eyes flared and she put one hand to her mouth, hiding the gasp of horror. Martha nodded, then shook her head and dropped back into the chair. "I have been aware that Lord Wellbridge's interest lay with you," she said, brokenly, "but I have not been able to help my heart. I have found myself eager for his company, determined to have it, to be good enough to gain it and yet, instead of that, Lord

Wellbridge has continually been drawn back towards you."

"You... you knew of that?" Emma barely noticed the tea tray set down by the maid, waving one hand vaguely to dismiss the maid without hesitation. "Even *I* did not know of that, Martha!"

Her sister let out a hard laugh.

"I can hardly believe that," she said, harshly. "No doubt you saw his interest, but you *also* saw how our mother and even our father encouraged *me* towards him. You were able to do nothing other than continue in your attentions toward him, hopeful that his interest would grow despite the attempts of our mother to push him toward me. Is that not so?"

Emma shook her head no, her sister's eyes narrowing in clear disbelief.

"It is as your sister says, Miss Fairley." Lord Yeatman's voice was gentle but held a steadiness to it which Emma appreciated. "She did not know. Yesterday afternoon, when Lord Wellbridge asked to speak to her, she presumed it was about *your* connection to him. She has spoken to me of Lord Wellbridge often, but it has always been in relation to you."

Martha said nothing as Emma reached for the tea pot, finding herself eager to do something rather than simply thinking about what her sister was saying. There came nothing but silence for the next few minutes, aside from the chinking of the China teapot on the teacups, though Emma's mind was whirring with confusing thoughts. Her sister had always known, had always believed, that Lord Wellbridge was interested in Emma's company, rather than her own, and yet had never said a single word? That did not make sense to Emma's mind, for surely if Martha had been as eager for Lord Wellbridge's attentions as Emma had believed, she would have spoken to Emma about her concerns!

"I had no knowledge of Lord Wellbridge's interest until yesterday, Martha." Picking up Martha's teacup, Emma set it down in front of her sister and then looked down, straight into her eyes. "Do you understand? I have not ever even considered him!"

Martha lifted her gaze and looked back into Emma's face. There were no tears in her eyes anymore, but her face was still flushed. She did not know whether or not Martha believed her, for the expression on her face was inscrutable.

"You said that you did not know of his interest until yesterday afternoon," Martha said slowly, as Emma turned to pour the tea for both herself and Lord Yeatman. "What does that mean?"

Picking up her teacup, Emma sat back down and, taking a sip of her tea, set her cup down again before she continued. Seeing how Martha had reacted to the mention of Lord Wellbridge and what she had said thus far, Emma's mind was whispering at her to be cautious and careful.

"You care for Lord Wellbridge, do you not?" Emma began, though with the silence that followed, it quickly became clear that Martha was not about to answer. "I speak the truth when I tell you that I did not know of his interest until it was much too late."

"What happened?" Martha's voice was crisp and

clear but also devoid of emotion. "How did you become aware of it?"

"Because," Emma said, choosing each word individually, "yesterday afternoon, he asked me to walk with him for a short while, though we would remain not far from Lord Yeatman and our mother. However, he asked me to sit in his carriage so that we might have a private conversation. I believed it was about you and, given that you are my sister, and given that you had been waiting for such a long time for his courtship, I agreed – albeit cautiously. What shocked me to my very core, however, was that once I sat in his carriage, he climbed in, pulled the door closed, and rapped on the roof so that we were both driven away together." Martha's face slowly began to drain of color. "Thereafter, he spoke to me about his supposed feelings," Emma continued, quietly. "I could not believe what I was hearing." Her sister closed her eyes, her chest heaving. "Lord Yeatman came to save me. If he had not, I believe that I would, very likely, have been forced into a marriage that I did not want, to a gentleman I did not care for. I am telling you this not because I want to injure you, Martha, but because I do not *want* you to be injured by him. This has truly shocked me, Martha. I was entirely unaware of his feelings and, in truth, even if I *had* been aware of them, I would not have permitted him to pursue me."

"I... I do not believe you."

"I do not care for him," Emma replied, fervently, though Martha's eyes remained steadfastly closed, her lips pursed. "Besides which, I would not have put you through any sort of pain, Martha. I could see that you were eager for his company and, though we are not close as sisters, though we are not friends as I had once hoped we would be, I would never have caused you unnecessary pain. I assure you that this is true, just as I speak it."

Martha finally opened her eyes and looked back steadily at Emma. She did not speak for some minutes, only to then shake her head and look away, her lips now pulled into a flat line.

"Given what Lord Wellbridge did, I spoke to him directly and stated that he was to effectively end the acquaintance between himself and all of you." Lord Yeatman reached and took Emma's hand for a moment, his eyes searching hers. "I hope that you understand why I said such a thing."

"Of course I do." Reassuring him, Emma offered him a small smile. "I am only sorry that you had cause to do it."

"Though you should not have spoken for me." Martha tossed her head, but Emma caught the glistening tears in her sister's eyes. "I could have made such a decision myself."

Emma and Lord Yeatman exchanged glances, though Lord Yeatman gave her only a tiny shrug, leaving the conversation in Emma's hands.

"It was said out of concern for you," she explained, simply. "Surely you cannot want to be in Lord Wellbridge's company again, not after hearing what I have told you about him?"

Martha sniffed but said nothing.

"I understand that you have fought for his attentions for a long time," Emma finished, an ache growing steadily in her heart as she prayed that her sister would understand that there was no malice in what Lord Yeatman had said to Lord Wellbridge. "But he is not worthy of you, Martha. He never was."

Her sister swallowed hard and then reached for her tea, still saying nothing.

"You fought for his attentions in more ways than one, did you not?"

Emma frowned, glancing at Lord Yeatman as he directed his words and his gaze toward Martha.

"I do not know what you mean." Martha lifted her chin, but her gaze continued to jump from Emma to Lord Yeatman and back again. "I think–"

"Yes, you do." Lord Yeatman shifted a little further forward in his chair, a frown encroaching on his brow. "*You* have been the one behind all of the incidents that have embarrassed your sister, have you not? *You* have been the one who made her fall, who knocked the arm of the footman, who, no doubt, paid a bribe to various footmen and maids to act in a particular fashion, so that your sister would appear at fault."

Emma snatched in a breath, her eyes flaring as she saw color begin to creep up into Martha's face.

"No, Martha," she breathed, as Martha's gaze dropped to her hands as they fiddled in her lap. "No, surely it could not be that *you*–"

"It was you, was it not?" Lord Yeatman interrupted, albeit with a gentle tone as his hand caught Emma's again. "Tell us the truth, Miss Fairley, if you will. It is only fair to your sister for her to know the truth. There is no sense in pretending, for I am already quite certain of the truth."

Emma, her throat tightening and her heart pounding, gazed at her sister, her voice breathless with shock and dread.

"Tell me the truth, Martha, please. Was it you? Are you the one who has been doing these things to me?"

Martha let out a long, slow breath and, closing her eyes, put out both hands and then let them fall.

"Yes," she said, eventually, her eyes opening to look directly back into Emma's face. "Yes, Emma. It was me."

CHAPTER TWENTY

Frederick's stomach kicked hard as Miss Martha Fairley made her confession. It was not that he was surprised that she had confirmed the thoughts that had come into his mind as he had listened to the exchange between the two sisters, but rather astonished at the very calm way in which she delivered this news. He could practically feel the shock running through Emma, for her hand had not only found him, but she had wound her fingers through his as well, gripping his hand hard as she stared straight ahead, looking only at her sister. His heart ached for her and, though he wanted to say something more, though he had questions he wanted to ask of her, Frederick chose to remain silent and let Emma speak, rather than letting loose with his questions.

"I cannot quite believe this." Emma closed her eyes tightly, her hand pressing his with such strength, it was almost a little painful. "You, Martha?" Opening her eyes, she looked back at her sister. "Why? Why would you do such things to me? I am your *sister*."

Martha's jaw tightened.

"It is because of Lord Wellbridge, sister," she said, with the very same calmness that had shocked Frederick before. "You said yourself that you saw that I cared for him, that I had an affection for him. Why, then, should I let my heart break when there was something I could do to garner Lord Wellbridge's attention?"

"By punishing me? Even though I did not know of his interest?" Emma asked, as the other Miss Fairley shrugged and looked away. "Why would you not simply speak to me? Why would you decide to treat me in such a way, instead of coming to me with an honest, gentle manner in which you would have been able to ascertain my *own* feelings on the matter?"

"Because I already knew them!" Martha rose to her feet, one finger shaking hard in Emma's direction, and it was all Frederick could do not to get to his feet and come between them. "I knew of your feelings. I knew that you were desperate to find a match, that you were utterly determined to secure a suitable husband, just as my own feelings were – and why then would you refuse Lord Wellbridge?"

"I did not even notice him!" Emma exclaimed as Frederick pressed her hand gently, reminding her of his presence, reminding her that he was there with her. "All I could think of, all I could see, was these embarrassments which kept overtaking me, these mortifications which had nothing to do with me and yet were placed at my feet! It is because of your actions that I became a wallflower!" Her hand pressed hard on Frederick's, the lady's voice wobbling as she continued to speak to her sister. "That night at the dinner table, when we dined with Lord and Lady Pleasance - Lord Wellbridge was not even present! Why then would you have the footman do such a thing as to make it look as though I was the reason for him dropping the plate?"

Martha sniffed.

"A bad reputation for clumsiness or the like does not come about simply by one action," she said, as Frederick closed his eyes, attempting to hold onto the ball of anger which was growing bigger with every word that came from Martha Fairley's lips. "I did not like that you were not only gaining the attention of Lord Wellbridge but also, even in your state as a wallflower, you were being noticed by one of the richest gentlemen in all of London!"

Frederick blinked, momentarily stunned.

"Wait a moment, Miss Fairley. You mean to say that you hoped that *I* would be pushed away from your sister simply because of her supposed clumsiness?" Seeing her nod and still utterly astonished by the lady's audacity and her complete lack of embarrassment as she admitted to these things, Frederick shook his head. "But why should you do that? Would you not be glad that I was seeking her company, rather than Lord Wellbridge?"

Martha let out a harsh, broken laugh which made the hair on Frederick's neck stand on end.

"Glad?" she repeated, scowling furiously. "Why should I be glad that my sister, my *younger* sister, has not only gained the attention of the one gentleman whom I have an interest in, but thereafter, once I have secured her status as a wallflower, finds herself with the attention of other gentlemen – the attention that *I* ought to have?" She flung up her hands. "The *ton* appears to have forgotten that *I* am the eldest! That *I* ought to be given precedence, that *I* ought to be looked at and considered before my younger sister. But no, they did not! I had Lord Wellbridge consider her over me, and that is the sole reason that I began my endeavors to bring about her ungainly reputation. It began at the end of last Season, and reached its successful conclusion at the beginning of this Season, only for *you*, Lord Yeatman, to step in. You were just as Lord Wellbridge was, seeing my sister rather than even once considering me! I thought, mayhap, that you were unaware of her reputation and thus, it was more than a little simple to continue with my plans. I gave a great deal of pin money to footmen and maids, I even resorted to a hair pin, and yet none of that made you even consider stepping away from her! Instead, it seemed to bring you all the closer and I–"

"Martha!"

Frederick started in surprise, as did Martha and Emma. He hastily got to his feet, only to see Lady Follet standing just inside the room, her eyes wide with shock and her face pale with fright.

"M...mama." Martha's demeanor changed in an instant, her eyes fixed on her mother, her hands clasped at her heart. "Mama, I do not know all that you have heard but–"

"I have heard enough to realize that Emma has always been telling us the truth," Lady Follet exclaimed, her voice cutting through Martha's excuses. "My goodness, can it be true? You would do such awful things to your sister simply because you were jealous of her?"

Martha lifted her chin.

"It was not jealousy. It was only that I desired society to see me first."

"I should take my leave." Frederick turned to Emma, aware that their fingers were still interlaced. "Would you be able to spare me a few minutes alone, Emma? I know it is a little improper but–"

"Of course." Emma rose to her feet, walking towards her mother and sister as Frederick hastened to the door. He did not want to linger in what was going to be a private family conversation, though, at the same time, he was relieved that the truth was now to be made known. Stepping out into the hallway, he waited a little anxiously for Emma's return, relieved when after only a few minutes, she stepped out to stand with him.

"My dear." The way that his heart leaped as he looked at her told Frederick that there was a good deal more to his affections than he had ever really considered. The desire to speak with her had come from only one particular thought: to beg her to accept his hand in marriage. There could be no delay.

"Are you quite all right?"

Taking her hand in his, they began to meander along the hallway – though quite where they were going, Frederick did not know, but nor did he care. All he wanted at present was to be in Emma's company.

"I am still a little stunned," she told him, her hazel eyes swirling with all manner of evident confusion, her face a little pale still. "I did not ever imagine that my sister would be the one doing such a thing to me, though I also did not imagine that Lord Wellbridge would have any sort of interest in me!"

Frederick smiled briefly.

"The latter does not come as a surprise to me, my dear Emma. The more that I have come to know you, the more my heart rejoices every time I am in your company. You are the most wonderful creature I have ever known."

She smiled and leaned against him, sighing heavily as their steps slowed, leaving them to stand together just outside the parlor door. Spying it, Frederick turned and, without a word, pushed it open and stepped inside.

Emma followed without a word.

Once the door was shut, Frederick turned, ready to open his arms to her – and she was already there, ready and waiting to be held tight. Frederick wrapped his arms around her, smelling honey and blossom as she clung to him, his heart aching both with love for her and also in sympathy for all she had endured. How long they stood together, Frederick did not know, but when she stepped back, he already felt it to be too short a time.

"You are sure that Lord Wellbridge will not do or say anything more?" she asked him, her voice soft with all the deep, overwhelming emotions that she felt. "You are quite certain that he will stay away from both me and my sister?"

Frederick's expression softened, his hand catching her chin gently.

"You are still concerned for Martha, even after what she has revealed to you?"

Emma nodded, though her eyes glistened with obvious tears.

"She is still my sister. Though I am saddened and sorrowful over what she has done, though my pain over that is still very great, I recall what Lord Wellbridge did to me, and my fear still lingers – both for myself and my sister."

"Then I can assure you that Lord Wellbridge will not come anywhere near you again," Frederick promised, finding himself a little overwhelmed with all that she had revealed to him. How precious she was! How wonderful! To have such a consideration within her over her sister, even after all that she had learned, was quite incredible. "I swear it."

"I thank you." Emma let out a slow sigh and then melted back into his arms. "Thank you for going to speak with him. I do not know what you said, but I trust your word."

Frederick could not help but drop a kiss on her forehead. When she looked up, startled, all he could do was smile. A gentle pink began to infuse her cheeks as she held his gaze and Frederick's heart began to quicken, fully aware of the desire deep within his heart.

"I want to marry you, Emma." The words came to him without hesitation and though they were plain and without excessive expression, he spoke them anyway. Emma's eyes rounded a little, though she began to smile, one hand lifting to press against his heart. "We have not been courting for long," Frederick continued, one shoulder lifting in a half-shrug, "but I do not consider that to be something that should hold us back. The truth is, Emma, the time that I have spent in your company has been more than enough to convince me that *you* are the only lady in all of England – in all of the world, no doubt – who could capture my heart."

"Your heart?" Her eyes widened all the more, the smile fading for a moment. "You care for me?"

Frederick shook his head, seeing the light flicker in her eyes.

"I do not just care for you, Emma. I believe I am falling in love with you."

She caught her breath and Frederick's heart squeezed with the sheer joy of what he was expressing to her, as though it was both relieved and delighted that he was finally telling her what had slowly been growing within him, ever since he had first set eyes on the lady.

"I am more convinced of it than ever," he continued, as Emma began to blink furiously, her eyes filling with what he hoped were tears of joy. "I want to marry you, Emma. I want to marry you not only to keep you safe, to keep you protected from Lord Wellbridge, but because I cannot even imagine my life without you being present in it. To consider my future as one without your bright smile, without your laughter, your kindness and your joy is nothing but a future of shadow and pain. You bring me such wondrous happiness that I can do nothing other than stand here before you and beg of you to accept my offer of matrimony. I swear to you that my heart is yours, and I shall fall more and more in love with you with every day that passes. I will give you all of myself, I will dedicate myself to my role as husband and I will prove my love to you every day of our lives… should you accept, that is."

Emma began to smile.

"My dear Yeatman, can you think for even a moment that I would refuse you?"

Hope leaped in his heart.

"When I was in the carriage with Lord Wellbridge, the only person I could think of was you," she told him, her other hand reaching up to wrap around his neck, her fingers brushing at his hair as sparks shot through him, his breath hitching. "My greatest fear was that I would be kept apart from you, that I would have no opportunity to return to the connection we had shared. I was afraid that Lord Wellbridge would take that from me, that he would steal every part of my future with you and break it into tiny little pieces, never again to be mended. But then," she continued, her voice dropping to a whisper, "*you* came to save me from him and in that moment, my future was restored. I have thought about you, and all that you have done for me and, as I search my heart, I discover that there is not only an affection there for you, but also love. I love you in return, Yeatman. It is an astonishing feeling, is it not?" She laughed as her other hand draped around his neck, the sound making Frederick beam with delight, though heat began to rise from his core as she pulled herself even closer to him. "To realize that one is in love is one thing, but to find that love returned is quite another."

"It *is* returned," Frederick assured her, beginning to lower his head as he looked deeply into her eyes and found nothing but love there. "Then you will marry me, Emma? You will be my bride?"

In answer, Emma pushed herself up on tiptoe and pressed her mouth to his. It was as though a torrent of water had broken over Frederick's frame, filling him with such warmth and yet such weakness at the strength of it. He kissed her back with as much fervency as he dared, aware of his heart screaming for joy at the happiness which now clung to them both.

"Yes, I shall marry you, Yeatman," she whispered, barely breaking the kiss, her eyes still closed. "I accept the offer of your hand in marriage. I *will* be your wife."

EPILOGUE

The moment that Emma had seen Lord Yeatman waiting for her at the front of the church, all her nervousness had fled. Even though the church was filled with friends, family and other noted guests, Emma was barely even aware of them. Lord Yeatman filled every part of her vision, and she could not look away from him.

"And now, Miss Emma Fairley, you make your vows."

The clergyman lifted an eyebrow and Emma nodded, having already heard Lord Yeatman's vows to her. She was more than ready to return them for all the words came from her heart.

"I take you to be my wedded husband, to have and to hold from this day forward, for better for worse, for richer, for poorer, in sickness and in health, to love, cherish, and to obey, till death us do part, according to God's holy ordinance."

Lord Yeatman pressed her hand, his eyes alight with the same joy that she herself felt within her heart. Had there not been such a solemnity about the ceremony, Emma felt as though she might jump up into his arms at this very moment, simply from sheer happiness.

"And now we come the giving and receiving of the ring."

Lord Yeatman nodded and, with a smile, took her hand and lifted it gently, before pushing the small, gold band onto the third finger of her left hand.

"Miss Emma Fairley," he murmured, "with this ring I thee wed. With my body I thee worship, and with all my worldly goods I thee endow."

Emma swallowed back the ache in her throat and the tears of joy as she looked down at her hand in his. It held a seal now, a promise that they would be man and wife for all the days of their life together. No-one could separate them now. She was his.

Lifting his hand by way of a blessing, the clergyman led them all in a final prayer.

"Eternal God, Creator and Preserver of all mankind, Giver of all spiritual grace, the Author of everlasting life: Send thy blessing upon these thy servants, this man and this woman, whom we bless in thy Name; that, as Isaac and Rebecca lived faithfully together, so these persons may surely perform and keep the vow and covenant between them made, whereof this Ring given and received is a token and pledge, and may ever remain in perfect love and peace together, and live according to thy laws; through Jesus Christ our Lord. Amen."

"Amen," Emma murmured, keeping her eyes closed for a little longer as the clergyman continued his blessing.

"Those whom God hath joined together let no man

put asunder. As these two here before you all have consented together in holy wedlock and have witnessed the same before God and this company, and thereto have given and pledged their troth either to other and have declared the same by giving and receiving of a Ring, and by joining of hands; I pronounce that they be Man and Wife together. In the Name of the Father, and of the Son, and of the Holy Ghost. Amen."

It was over. Emma could hardly take it in, feeling as though she were walking on air as Lord Yeatman led her away from the congregation and through a door to a small room where they were to sign their names to the marriage certificate and the church register. Once that was completed, the clergyman instructed them both to take their leave of the church and to step outside, where friends and family would now be waiting with their cries of congratulations.

"A moment, Emma?"

Lord Yeatman turned to face her as the clergyman made his way back through the church, giving them a few moments alone.

"Yes?"

His eyes held a trace of worry and Emma frowned gently.

"Are you happy?"

Her eyebrows flew towards her hairline.

"Happy?" she repeated, as he nodded. "Yeatman, I am overjoyed!"

A smile blossomed at once and Emma laughed, doing just as she had longed to do some minutes before and throwing herself into his arms. He held her tightly as she wrapped her arms around his neck, still barely able to take in that they were now man and wife.

"I am overjoyed," she repeated, as she leaned back just a little, seeing him smile. "This day has been more wonderful, more glorious than I could ever have imagined. I am your wife now, Yeatman, and there is nothing I have wanted more."

Lord Yeatman bent his head and kissed her lightly, the heat of his lips rushing straight through her so that she sighed against him when he lifted his head.

"I am glad to hear it," he said softly as Emma smiled back at him. "To hear you make those vows, to know that I am now your husband brings me such delight, I can barely speak of it. It is too much for me to express."

"That is exactly how I feel."

He kissed her again and this time, it was long and lingering, leaving her heart pounding and her breathing ragged. Lord Yeatman chuckled softly as heat seared Emma's cheeks.

"We should go out to everyone waiting," he said softly, though he did not drop his arms from her waist or make any attempt to move back. "They will be expecting us."

Emma sighed softly, desiring nothing more than to linger here, alone with Lord Yeatman.

"Yes, I suppose we should."

His head lowered and he caught her lips for a third time, though this time it was only for a moment.

"I love you, Emma. I shall always love you, no matter what happens."

Emma put one hand to his cheek, searching his eyes as her heart swelled with affection for him, all over again.

"And I shall love you," she promised, softly. "I shall love you every day for the rest of my life."

I am glad that Emma and Lord Yeatman finally got their happy ever after!

The next book in the series is now on preorder! Check it out at this link. The Determined Wallflower

Did you miss the first book in the Wallflower series? The Wallflower's Unseen Charm Read ahead for a preview!

MY DEAR READER

Thank you for reading and supporting my books! I hope this story brought you some escape from the real world into the always captivating Regency world. A good story, especially one with a happy ending, just brightens your day and makes you feel good! If you enjoyed the book, would you leave a review on Amazon? Reviews are always appreciated.

Below is a complete list of all my books! Why not click and see if one of them can keep you entertained for a few hours?

The Duke's Daughters Series
The Duke's Daughters: A Sweet Regency Romance Boxset
A Rogue for a Lady
My Restless Earl
Rescued by an Earl
In the Arms of an Earl
The Reluctant Marquess (Prequel)

A Smithfield Market Regency Romance
The Smithfield Market Romances: A Sweet Regency Romance Boxset
The Rogue's Flower

Saved by the Scoundrel
Mending the Duke
The Baron's Malady

The Returned Lords of Grosvenor Square
The Returned Lords of Grosvenor Square: A Regency Romance Boxset
The Waiting Bride
The Long Return
The Duke's Saving Grace
A New Home for the Duke

The Spinsters Guild
The Spinsters Guild: A Sweet Regency Romance Boxset
A New Beginning
The Disgraced Bride
A Gentleman's Revenge
A Foolish Wager
A Lord Undone

Convenient Arrangements
Convenient Arrangements: A Regency Romance Collection
A Broken Betrothal
In Search of Love
Wed in Disgrace
Betrayal and Lies
A Past to Forget
Engaged to a Friend

Landon House

Landon House: A Regency Romance Boxset
Mistaken for a Rake
A Selfish Heart
A Love Unbroken
A Christmas Match
A Most Suitable Bride
An Expectation of Love

Second Chance Regency Romance
Second Chance Regency Romance Boxset
Loving the Scarred Soldier
Second Chance for Love
A Family of her Own
A Spinster No More

Soldiers and Sweethearts
Soldiers and Sweethearts Boxset
To Trust a Viscount
Whispers of the Heart
Dare to Love a Marquess
Healing the Earl
A Lady's Brave Heart

Ladies on their Own: Governesses and Companions
Ladies on their Own Boxset
More Than a Companion
The Hidden Governess
The Companion and the Earl
More than a Governess
Protected by the Companion

Lost Fortunes, Found Love
Lost Fortunes, Found Love Boxset
A Viscount's Stolen Fortune
For Richer, For Poorer
Her Heart's Choice
A Dreadful Secret
Their Forgotten Love
His Convenient Match

Only for Love
The Heart of a Gentleman
A Lord or a Liar
The Earl's Unspoken Love
The Viscount's Unlikely Ally
The Highwayman's Hidden Heart
Miss Millington's Unexpected Suitor

Waltzing with Wallflowers
The Wallflower's Unseen Charm
The Wallflower's Midnight Waltz
Wallflower Whispers
The Ungainly Wallflower
The Determined Wallflower
The Wallflower's Secret (Revenge of the Wallflowers series)

Christmas Stories
The Uncatchable Earl
Love and Christmas Wishes: Three Regency Romance Novellas
A Family for Christmas

Mistletoe Magic: A Regency Romance
Heart, Homes & Holidays: A Sweet Romance Anthology

Christmas Kisses Series
Christmas Kisses Box Set
The Lady's Christmas Kiss
The Viscount's Christmas Queen
Her Christmas Duke

Happy Reading!
    All my love,
    Rose

A SNEAK PEEK OF THE WALLFLOWER'S UNSEEN CHARM

PROLOGUE

"You must promise me that you will *try*."

Miss Joy Bosworth rolled her eyes at her mother.

"Try to be more like my elder sisters, yes? That *is* what you mean, is it not?"

"And what is wrong with being like them?" Lady Halifax's stern tone told Joy in no uncertain terms that to criticize Bettina, Sarah, and Mary – all three of whom had married within the last few years – was a very poor decision indeed. Wincing, Joy fell silent and dropped her gaze to her lap as her beleaguered lady's maid continued to fix her hair. This was the third time that her lady's maid had set her hair, for the first two attempts had been deemed entirely unsuitable by Joy's mother – though quite what was wrong with it, Joy had been completely unable to see.

"You are much too forward, too quick to give your opinion," her mother continued, gazing at Joy's reflection in the looking glass, her eyes narrowing a little. "All of your elder sisters are quiet, though Bettina perhaps a little too much so, but their husbands greatly appreciate that about them! They speak when they are asked to speak, give their opinion when it is desired and otherwise say very little when it comes to matters which do not concern them. *You,* on the other hand, speak when you are *not* asked to do so, give your opinion most readily, and say a great deal on *any* subject even when it does not concern you!"

Hearing the strong emphasis, Joy chose not to drop her head further, as her mother might have expected, but instead to lift her chin and look back steadily. She was not about to be cowed when it came to such a trait. In some ways, she was rather proud of her determination to speak as she thought, for she was the only one of her sisters who did so. Mayhap it was simply because she was the youngest, but Joy did not truly know why - she had always been determined to speak up for herself and, simply because she was in London, was not, she thought, cause to alter herself now!

"You must find a suitable husband!" Exclaiming aloud, Lady Halifax threw up her hands, perhaps seeing the glint of steel in Joy's eyes. "Continuing to behave as you are will not attract anyone to you, I can assure you of that!"

"The *right* gentleman would still be attracted," Joy shot back, adding her own emphasis. "There must be some amongst society who do not feel the same way as you, Mother. I do not seek to disagree with you, only to suggest that there might be a little more consideration in some, or even a different viewpoint altogether!"

"I know what I am talking about!" Lady Halifax smote Joy gently on the shoulder though her expression was one of frustration. "I have already had three daughters wed and it would do you well to listen to me and my advice."

Joy did not know what to say. Yes, she had listened to her mother on many an occasion, but that did not mean that she had to take everything her mother said to heart... and on this occasion, she was certain that Lady Halifax was quite wrong.

"If I am not true to who I am, Mama, then will that not make for a very difficult marriage?"

"A difficult marriage?" This was said with such a degree of astonishment that Joy could not help but smile. "There is no such thing as a difficult marriage, not unless one of the two parties *within* the marriage itself attempts to make it so. Do you not understand, Joy? I am telling you to alter yourself so that you do *not* cause any difficulties, both for yourself now, and for your husband in the future."

The smile on Joy's face slipped and then blew away, her forehead furrowing as she looked at her mother again. Lady Halifax was everything a lady of quality ought to be, and she had trained each of her daughters to be as she was... except that Joy had never been the success her other daughters had been. Even now, the thought of stepping into marriage with a gentleman she barely knew, simply because he was deemed suitable, was rather horrifying to Joy, and was made all the worse by the idea that she would somehow have to pretend to be someone she was not!

"As I have said, Joy, you will try."

This time, Joy realized, it was not a question her mother had been asking her but a statement. A statement which said that she was expected to do nothing other than what her mother said – and to do so without question also.

I shall not lie.

"I think my hair is quite presentable now, Mama." Steadfastly refusing to either agree with or refuse what her mother had said, Joy sat up straight in her chair, her head lifting, her shoulders dropping low as she turned her head from side to side. "Very elegant, I must say."

"The ribbon is not the right color."

Joy resisted the urge to roll her eyes for what would be the second time.

"Mama, it is a light shade of green and it is threaded through the many braids Clara has tied my hair into. It is quite perfect and cannot be faulted. Besides, it does match the gown perfectly. You made certain of that yourself."

So saying, she threw a quick smile to her lady's maid and saw a twitch of Clara's lips before the maid bowed her head, stepping back so that Lady Halifax would not see the smile on her face.

"It is not quite as I would want it, but it will have to do." Lady Halifax sniffed and waved one hand in Clara's direction. "My daughter requires her gown now. And be quick about it, we are a little short on time."

"If you had not insisted that Clara do my hair on two further occasions, then we would not be in danger of being tardy," Joy remarked, rising from her chair, and walking across the room, quite missing the flash in her mother's eyes. "It was quite suitable the first time."

"*I* shall be the judge of that," came the sharp retort, as Lady Halifax stalked to the door. "Now do hurry up. The carriage is waiting, and I do not want us to bring the attention of the entire *ton* down upon us by walking in much later than any other!"

Joy sighed and nodded, turning back to where Clara was ready with her gown. Coming to London and seeking out a suitable match was not something she could get the least bit excited about, and this ball, rather than being a momentous one, filled with hope and expectation, felt like a heaviness on her shoulders. The sooner it was over, Joy considered, the happier she would be.

CHAPTER ONE

"And Lord Granger is seated there."

"Mm-hm."

Nudging Joy lightly, her mother scowled.

"You are not paying the least bit of attention! Instead, you are much too inclined towards staring! Though quite what you are staring at, I cannot imagine!"

Joy tilted her head but did not take her eyes away from what she had been looking at.

"I was wondering whether that lady there – the one with the rather ornate hairstyle – found it difficult to wear such a thing without difficulty or pain." The lady in question had what appeared to be a bird's nest of some description, adorned with feathers and lace, planted on one side of her head, with her hair going through it as though it were a part of the creation. There was also a bird sitting on the edge of the nest, though to Joy's eyes, it looked rather monstrous and not at all as it ought. "Surely it must be stuck to her head in some way." She could not keep a giggle back when the lady curtsied and then rose, only for her magnificent headpiece to wobble terribly. "Oh dear, perhaps it is not as well secured as it ought to be!"

"Will you stop speaking so loudly?"

The hiss from Lady Halifax had Joy's attention snapping back to her mother, a slight flush touching the edge of her cheeks as she realized that one or two of the other ladies near them were glancing in her direction. She had spoken a little too loudly for both her own good and her mother's liking.

"My apologies, Mama."

"I should think so!" Lady Halifax grabbed Joy's arm in a somewhat tight grip and then began to walk in the opposite direction of that taken by the lady with the magnificent hair. "Pray do not embarrass both me and yourself, with your hasty tongue!"

"I do not mean to," Joy muttered, allowing her mother to take her in whatever direction she wished. "I simply speak as I think."

"A trait I ought to have worked out of you by now, but instead, it seems determined to cling to you!" With a sigh, Lady Halifax shook her head. "Now look, do you see there?"

Coming to a hasty stop, Joy looked across the room, following the direction of her mother's gaze. "What is it that you wish me to look at, Mama?"

"Those young ladies there," came the reply. "Do you see them? They stand clustered together, hidden in the shadows of the ballroom. Even their own mothers or sponsors have given up on them!"

A frown tugged at Joy's forehead.

"I do not know what you are speaking of Mama."

"The wallflowers!" Lady Halifax turned sharply to Joy, her eyes flashing. "Do you not see them? They stand there, doing nothing other than adorning the wall. They are passed over constantly, ignored by the gentlemen of the *ton,* who care very little for their company."

"Then that is the fault of the gentlemen of the *ton,*" Joy answered, a little upset by her mother's remarks. "I do not think it is right to blame the young ladies for such a thing."

Lady Halifax groaned aloud, closing her eyes.

"Why do you willfully misunderstand? They are not wallflowers by choice, but because they are deemed as unsuitable for marriage, for one reason or another."

"Which, again, might not be their own doing."

"Perhaps, but all the same," Lady Halifax continued, sounding more exasperated than ever, "I have shown you these young ladies as a warning."

Joy's eyebrows shot towards her hairline.

"A warning?"

"Yes, that you will yourself become one such young lady if you do not begin to behave yourself and act as you ought." Moving so that she faced Joy directly, Lady Halifax narrowed her eyes a little. "You will find yourself standing there with them, doing nothing other than watching the gentlemen of London take various *other* young ladies out to dance, rather than showing any genuine interest in you. Would that not be painful? Would that not trouble you?"

The answer her mother wished her to give was evident to Joy, but she could not bring herself to say it. It was not that she wanted to cause her mother any pain, but that she could not permit herself to be false, not even if it would bring her a little comfort.

"It might," she admitted, eventually, as Lady Halifax let out another stifled groan, clearly exasperated. "But as I have said before, Mama, I do not wish to be courted by a gentleman who is unaware of my true nature. I do not see why I should hide myself away, simply so that I can please a suitor. If such a thing were to happen, if I were to be willing to act in that way, it would not make for a happy arrangement. Sooner or later, my real self would return to the fore, and then what would my husband do? It is not as though he could step back from our marriage. Therefore, I would be condemning both him and myself, to a life of misery. I do not think that would be at all agreeable."

"That is where you are wrong." Lady Halifax lifted her chin, though she looked straight ahead. "To be wed is the most satisfactory situation one can find oneself in, regardless of the circumstances. It is not as though you will spend a great deal of time with your husband so, therefore, you will never need to reveal your 'true nature', as you put it."

The more her mother talked, the more Joy found herself growing almost despondent, such was the picture Lady Halifax was painting of what would be waiting for her. She understood that yes, she was here to find a suitable match, but to then remove to her husband's estate, where she would spend most of her days alone and only be in her husband's company whenever he desired it, did not seem to Joy to be a very pleasant circumstance. That would be very dull indeed, would it not? Her existence would become small, insignificant, and utterly banal, and that was certainly *not* the future Joy wanted for herself.

"Now, do lift your head up, stand tall, and smile," came the command. "We must go and speak to Lord Falconer and Lord Dartford at once."

Joy hid her sigh by lowering her head, her eyes squeezing closed for a few moments. There was no time to protest, however, no time to explain to her mother that what had just been discussed had settled Joy's mind against such things as this, for Lady Halifax once more marched Joy across the room and, before she knew it, introduced Joy to the two gentlemen whom she had pointed out, as well as to one Lady Dartford, who was Lord Dartford's mother.

"Good evening." Joy rose from her curtsey and tried to smile, though her smile was a little lackluster. "How very glad I am to make your acquaintance."

"Said quite perfectly." Lord Dartford chuckled, his dark eyes sweeping across her features, then dropping down to her frame as Joy blushed furiously. "So, you are next in line to try your hand at the marriage mart?"

"Next in line?"

"Yes." Lord Dartford waved a hand as though to dismiss her words and her irritation, which Joy had attempted to make more than evident by the sweep of her eyebrow. "You have three elder sisters do you not?"

"Yes, I do." Joy kept her eyebrows lifted. "All of whom are all now wed and settled."

"And now you must do the same." Lord Dartford chuckled, but Joy did not smile. The sound was not a pleasant one. "Unfortunately, none of your sisters were able to catch my eye and, alas, I do not think that you will be able to do so either."

"Dartford!"

His mother's gasp of horror was clear, but Joy merely smiled, her stomach twisting at the sheer arrogance which the gentleman had displayed.

"That is a little forward of you, Lord Dartford," she remarked, speaking quite clearly, and ignoring the way that her mother set one hand to the small of her back in clear warning. "What is to say that I would have any interest in *your* company?"

This response wiped the smile from Lord Dartford's face. His dark eyes narrowed, and his jaw set but, much to Joy's delight, his friend began to guffaw, slapping Lord Dartford on the shoulder.

"You have certainly been set in your place!" Lord Falconer laughed as Joy looked back into Lord Dartford's angry expression without flinching. "And the lady is quite right, that was one of the most superior things I have heard you say this evening!"

"Only this evening?" Enjoying herself far too much, Joy tilted her head and let a smile dance across her features. "Again, Lord Dartford, I ask you what difference it would make to me to have a gentleman such as yourself interested in furthering their acquaintance with me? It is not as though I must simply accept every gentleman who comes to seek me out, is it? And I can assure you, I certainly would not accept you!"

Lord Falconer laughed again but Lord Dartford's

eyes narrowed all the more, his jaw tight and his frame stiff with clear anger and frustration.

"I do not think a young lady such as yourself should display such audacity, Miss Bosworth."

"And if I want your opinion, Lord Dartford, then I will ask you for it," Joy shot back, just as quickly. "Thus far, I do not recall doing so."

"We must excuse ourselves."

The hand that had been on Joy's back now turned into a pressing force that propelled her away from Lord Dartford, Lord Falconer, and Lady Dartford – the latter of whom was standing, staring at Joy with wide eyes, her face a little pale.

"Do excuse us."

Lady Halifax inclined her head and then took Joy's hand, grasping it tightly rather than with any gentleness whatsoever, dragging her away from the gentlemen she had only just introduced Joy to.

"Mama, you are hurting me!" Pulling her hand away, Joy scowled when her mother rounded on her. "Please, you must stop–"

"Do you know what you have done?"

The hissed words from her mother had Joy stopping short, a little surprised at her mother's vehemence.

"I have done nothing other than speak my mind and set Lord Dartford – someone who purports to be a gentleman – back into his place. I do not know what makes him think that I would have *any* interest in–"

"News of this will spread through London!" Lady Halifax blinked furiously, and it was only then that Joy saw the tears in her mother's eyes. "This is your very first ball on the eve of your come out, and you decide to speak with such force and impudence to the Earl of Dartford?"

A writhing began to roll itself around Joy's stomach.

"I do not know what you mean. I did nothing wrong."

"It is not about wrong or right," came the reply, as Lady Halifax whispered with force towards Joy. "It is about wisdom. You did not speak with any wisdom this evening, and now news of what you did will spread throughout society. Lady Dartford will see to that."

Joy lifted her shoulders and then let them fall.

"I could not permit Lord Dartford to speak to me in such a way. I am worthy of respect, am I not?"

"You could have ignored him!" Lady Halifax threw up her hands, no longer managing to maintain her composure, garnering the attention of one or two others nearby. "You did not have to say a single thing! A simple look – or a slight curl of the lip – would have sufficed. Instead, you did precisely what I told you not to do and now news of your audacity will spread through London. Lady Dartford is one of the most prolific gossips in all of London and given that you insulted her son, I fear for what she will say."

Joy kept her chin lifted.

"Mama, Lady Dartford was shocked at her own son's remarks to me."

"But that does not mean that she will speak of *him* in the same way that she will speak of you," Lady Halifax told her, a single tear falling as red spots appeared on her cheeks. "Do you not understand, Joy?"

"Lord Falconer laughed at what I said."

Lady Halifax closed her eyes.

"That means nothing, other than the fact that he found your remarks and your behavior to be mirthful. It will not save your reputation."

"I did nothing to ruin my reputation."

"Oh, but you did." A flash came into her mother's eyes. "You may not see it as yet, but I can assure you, you have done yourself a great deal of damage. I warned you, I *asked* you to be cautious and instead, you did the opposite. Now, within the first ball of the Season, your sharp tongue and your determination to speak as you please has brought you into greater difficulty than you can imagine." Her eyes closed, a heavy sigh breaking from her. "Mayhap you will become a wallflower after all."

Hmm, my mother always said my mouth would get me into trouble...and now Miss Bosworth could be in trouble! Check out the rest of the story on the Kindle store The Wallflower's Unseen Charm

JOIN MY MAILING LIST

Sign up for my newsletter to stay up to date on new releases, contests, giveaways, freebies, and deals!

Free book with signup!

Monthly Facebook Giveaways! Books and Amazon gift cards!
Join me on Facebook: https://www.facebook.com/rosepearsonauthor

Website: www.RosePearsonAuthor.com

Follow me on Goodreads: Author Page

Printed in Great Britain
by Amazon